T0063364

Three Days To Life

Three Days To Life

Antarix Bhardwaj

PARTRIDGE

A Penguin Random House Company

To order additional copies of this book, contact
Partridge India
000 800 10062 62
orders.india@partridgepublishing.com

www.partridgepublishing.com/india

My Dad, Mom, Anu, Suyash
Deepak

Contents

ACKNOWLEDGEMENTS

This is my first book and I have too many people to thank, as I was supported by many, directly and indirectly. First of all thanks to my friend Deepak, I don't know whether he remembers this or not when he said to me, "You are different from all others because you can create." These words made me believe that I can write. Thanks Deepak for being with me these all years.

The journey to anything is possible if we are supported by a true friend, who will stand for you when you can't, who will push you when you are about to give up, who will fight for you when you are tired, and at last will leave you alone on the road when she thinks you can handle it from now. Thanks Ankita for being that friend to me in the journey to this book. Whenever I use to run out of ideas, get distracted, confused or demoralized I use to go to Ankita, most of the times she did not even knew that I am asking for help, but her words were full of solutions. Thanks for being with me during this journey.

A brother is enough with you when you need to fight the world; luckily I had two Suyash and Parshant. They trusted me when I had lost the trust in me, thanks would be a small word for both of you.

Anu who had almost every time contradicted me and because of that today I could accept and appreciate people of different nature around me.

Anuj and Vikas friends I have ever wanted. Anuj had always supported me blindly in anything I had done in last year and Vikas had always shown me the right direction. Thanks for the support guys or in the words of Vikas salute to both of you.

At last my friend who were and will always be with be Gaurav, Meenakshi, Jayant, Zeeshan, Kuntal, Vishnu, Tanishka, Chandra, Simran, thank you guys, you all are life to me, thanks for your support.

1

The Old Road

*I*t is sharp 02:00 hours, a serpent road ahead and miles behind. Road, which is cut from giant mountains and runs around them, between them and few a times across them via deep cut dark tunnels. Road at height of more than 2000m above sea level accompanied with its two confidants, who had made so far with it, they stood with it, when road stands and ran when the road ran. A deep valley covered with oak and pine trees on one side of the road and irregularly perpendicular cut mountain rocks covered with grass and loose stones on another.

The road is covered with fresh water from the clouds. The Clouds are in colors and seems to be another companion of road from last few days. Clouds have settled on road and floats above it in such a way that it seems to the people from far that this road is built in sky between the clouds.

Clouds are the naughtiest among all four, they do what so ever they feel like they rain heavily when they feel like or they don't or they may be in a mood to drizzle, hail, snow, what so ever pleases them. And when they are in a mood to show their strength they pour water in such a quantity that they cause big rocks to move, uproot trees, houses or anything in this world.

The full moon is three nights from now, but the light from moon is still illuminating the valley. The naughty clouds seem to be in the mood to play, they are not allowing moon to shine in full. But what so ever light of moon manages to reach the valley, it adds to the beauty of road. The light from moon make the clouds look white like pearls spread around and over the road. And free flowing cold breeze make pearls flows here and there.

When someone says that:

"The road was beautiful than its destination."

They must be talking about a road like this.

This road is hardly travelled by anyone at this time, as the road is not in best of its grip. A mistake may take a traveler to deep valley on one side of road or to mountain rocks on another, what happens to the traveler after that is another part of story, which depends on many factors such as place of mishap, grip of tires, reaction time of traveler, vehicle traveler is driving and a lot more. If I write them all, I will be needing few more pages, so to be short and precise I will like to keep the way we call it 'luck,' i.e. what happens to the traveler next depends on his luck.

No traffic, no people but a barren road, all birds and animals safe in their house, and having a great sleep. Only road with two of its confidants and clouds, clouds which are being controlled with cold breeze, presently are awake. Besides dark it's not silent here, the mellifluous sound of water drops falling from trees could be heard at some places or the roar of water running from the mountains and making its way down to valley at some other places or the sound of small pebbles which are made loose because of rain and running water falling on road from mountains and even the furious breeze is loud enough to be heard.

The valley, the clouds, the road, the wind, the rain, all this may look lifeless but it is the best art of nature painted on the canvas, hardly any movement and everything seems to be painted so beautifully that, it may not look to have life but soul is eminent.

Suddenly the life to this portrait is provided by the dark color car that dashes through the road, it flew through the clouds and vanishes ahead in them. But the back rare view lights of car are still visible, losing their intensity as the car travels ahead.

"The roads are playgrounds for many,
but become perpetual tracks for
those who try to trace them."

These lines are taking shape for Mr. Dixit. Dixit a young entrepreneur and director of a five and half year old sports goods company named Unite Sports. A handsome and smart man of age 26 is on the way to Shimla from Srinagar. Srinagar is the capital city of Kashmir, Kashmir which is known as 'heaven on earth' and now heading towards Shimla, a beautiful city which is also known as 'The queen of hill stations'. Actually he is heading towards Shimla as he has some business meeting the coming evening there.

The road from the capital of 'heaven on earth' to 'the queen of hill stations' is blessed with clouds, which had made Anant late than he expected. The clouds have snowed at few places, hailed on some others and just rained at rest. With less visibility because of clouds and less grip because of wet road he could not move with the speed he wanted to, but then too he is doing fine in case of speed with his dark color BMW X3 (F25).

Now and then Dixit is staring at watch, may be because he is getting late or maybe he just wants this night to pass. It does not need a special art to figure out from his eyes that he is running low in his sleeping hours and tension in his eyes is point of attraction of his face. He had ignored all of the best scenic masterpieces on the way which he had enjoyed in his last trips, the places on the road where he took halt and spent time with valleys and enjoyed the sound of silence. But this time all those places did not existed at all on the way for him.

He pulls all glasses of his car up, as clouds shows their presence with the snow. Suddenly his mobile which is placed on the side seat glow to life and his reflexes came into play, he slows the car and a slight hint of smile on his face is visible. It seems it is the call he was waiting for and the reason for which he is so messed up is going to be resolved. He took the mobile but all the hopes lost in a fraction of second as he founds that the light of the mobile was an indication of low battery.

Looking at low battery message on his mobile Mr. Dixit's face gets decorated with a big smile, but at this time by a forceful one. He plugs his mobile to the charger and places his foot on the accelerator. And his car dashes into the clouds ahead.

2

The Dawn

*I*t's burning morning, with sun in best of its colors, holding his position right on the top in the sky and like a ruthless ruler showing no mercy on anyone, just heating and burning everything in the way. The temperature has crossed 42 degree Celsius, and hovering near to 43. The temperature is enough to faint you with heat stock and not just the sun, but adding to the charm of summers in Delhi, hot wind called loo is blowing, which have potential to make you low on glucose and collapse you like house of cards in few minutes. It is mid-June and during this period of year, Delhi burns with heat, and is almost like a furnace to people leaving here.

Time is tickling slowly for Anant; last few minutes were like an hour to him. He is standing under the bus stop shed, which besides been painted in green is hardly protecting him from sun. It's early ten in morning and

Anant is waiting for his regular bus to his small office, which is less an office and more a godown.

Anant is a young entrepreneur, 21 of age, who had just started a business that deals with sports goods, in partnership with his friend. The business is just four months old but Anant and his partner are doing great work. Besides being young and armature to this field, they are earning a fair amount to make their leaving.

Waiting is the most boring thing to do and when you are drained in sweat and you have to wipe the sweat from your face in every quarter minute, waiting becomes the most difficult job.

Anant removes his handkerchief from his trouser, wipes sweat from his face with it and looks at the watch on his wrist, it's almost time for the bus but no bus is seen on the road. He is eagerly looking for the bus as he has to finish many tasks in the office. He is making a list in his mind of the tasks which he have to finish today, his face again gets covered with the sweat and he wipes it with his handkerchief again.

Sweltered in sweat, Anant is waiting for his bus, his eyes at the road from where the bus is expected but again alike last few days, before the bus arrives, a young and pretty girl is walking towards the bus stop. She is dressed in pink sleeveless top, Capri and with black shades on her face, she looks so attractive that Anant tries to take his vision away but could not.

As she came closer she looks at Anant and he immediately looks back on the road pretending as if he is looking for the bus. She came and stood under the shed of bus stop, right next to Anant. She looks at Anant and passes a smile; this is the first time in last few days she smiled and Anant who is looking at her with side eye, is glad from inside to see her smiling. But Anant did not know how to react and he avoids her by keep looking in the direction from where bus is accepted. His weird look made her to react in same ignorant way as he did.

After some time bus came for which Anant is waiting, the doors opened, Anant stepped in the bus and doors shut after him, he dint had a look at her since then. But she watched this arrogant man carrying his ass away. When the bus started to move, Anant turned back and look back at her. He is not able to justify his own behavior to himself, and on the way he is thinking about that girl and his behavior towards her.

This is a new fresh morning at bus stop and sun as usual at its best making Anant to sweat, Anant is again waiting for the bus to his office, but this time instead of business worries or the tasks he had to complete today, he is thinking of that girl, besides he tried his best not to think of her but sometimes, few things are not in hand.

Again it's time for the bus and Anant is looking in the direction from which bus is accepted, but today his eyes are not searching for the bus on the road but they are searching for that girl on the pavement.

Luck is running in Anant's favor, he saw her coming. Today she is dressed in dark color shirt with her hairs pulled back but left loose, a dark color tapered knee length skirt and adding to the mesmerizing beauty of her were pumps with two inch heels. Anant is totally drowned in her as he is staring at her with his eyes open wide at her, while she is moving towards him. When she came close, he diverts his eyes and starts to look on road for the bus. She came and stood at her usual place, next to him.

Anant wants to apologize for his behavior, but something is stopping him, may be its pride or maybe he lacked confidence. But at last he collects all confidence that he has, kills his pride and makes a decision to talk to her as he do not want to spend another day thinking of her, as he had spent his last day.

Anant thought on it for a while and finally he wears a fake smile on his face, looks at his cloths finding all fine he turns towards her with the full on sprit to talk to her, but always luck does not remain in favor, she is talking at her mobile phone and looking in other direction. His confidence scatters and smile is vanishes, but keeping his hopes high he decides to talk when she will be done with her call. So now, all he need to do is to wait for her call to get finish, but before her call gets finish his bus arrives.

He boards the bus, and as the bus starts to move, he took a pause on the stairs of bus and smiles at himself. He could not believe what he was going to do. He whispers to himself, "I was carried with the thoughts." And he smiles wider.

Few more days passed but with no change. Anant is normal now he is out of her thoughts, but every morning when she came to bus stop something unusual happens at that movement to Anant, which he himself could not explain. He felt like talking to her but never did. Few a times she looks at him but whenever eye clashes he ignores or pretends that he was looking at some other thing. But when he is at his office he is focused at his work, no thoughts of her bother him, like the first day.

Another morning and the monopoly of sun over the earth seem to be ending today. The clouds are making rounds, the sky is now dominated by them, and they are hardly giving any chance to sun to show its fury. The temperature is friendly near to thirty degree Celsius and like usual days Anant is standing at the bus stop, waiting for the bus to his office.

Anant is looking at the road for his bus. The clouds starts to roar and lightning is seen in the sky. The clouds seems to be in a mood to party, the music caused by thunder is loud and happening, this is what people wants to hear from too long. And suddenly the most awaited party begins the rain drops started to dance on the ground. The sound of heavy rain is melodious then any music and petrichor is sweeter than any cologne.

People, who were under the sky, are taken by heavy rain by surprise, they ran to take shed, and the bus stop is filled in seconds. Most of the people are not prepared for rain, hence are with nothing to protect them from rain. But unlike others Anant knew from today's Newspaper that it would rain today so he is prepared and carrying an umbrella.

Anant is waiting for his bus to office like usual days and again like usual days before the bus arrives the same girl is visible, but this time she is not walking but running towards the bus stop with what so ever speed she could manage.

She is not carrying an umbrella to protect her from rain, but she is using her hand bag to protect her head and face from rain, but it is hardly of any use. She is already drenched in water completely. She is wearing a deep blue color top and black color skirt, but the wet top too is looking black due to water. Beauty, elegance, charisma is oozing out from her and Anant is helplessly looking at her.

She ran under the bus stop shed, the shed is almost jam-packed but she manages to find some space and stands right next to Anant. Standing next to Anant she is trying to manage her wet hair by tying them but in doing so water is sprinkling on Anant's shirt, but he is hardly minding it. She ties her hair in a bun and her face is looking more clear and pretty with her hairs tied in a bun.

While she is busy in making herself comfortable and wiping water from her cloths, Anant is looking at her with his eyes open wide. He tried to look away but she is looking so pretty that he could not. He can feel the force from within, which is forcing him to talk to her but he is not finding the way to start the conversation.

Anant is looking at her and finds that she is not able to handle her hand bag while wiping water from her cloths. He thought it's time to act like a gentle man and ask her to hand over her hand bag for a while so she can continue wiping water from her cloths smoothly. But he dint asked as he thought she may consider him freak. The strips of her handbag are slipping from her shoulder now and then, she turns towards Anant and smiles, Anant smiles in return, she pulls her hairs back which are in front of her face left loose from bun and says:

"Can you please hold my bag for a while I am unable to manage it."

Luck seems to be showering these days on Anant, she herself had started the conversation. Without any word Anant forwards his hand and takes her handbag with a smile and she continues with her cleaning process. Anant is watching her, she removes her bellies and left them a side so that water may drip from them, then she twists her feet to relive from pain that she had gained while she was running.

Anant could see water making its way from her cheeks to neck and then gets absorbed by her top. She looks back at Anant, smiles and forwards her hand asking for her hand bag, Anant hands over her bag. She smiles wider in return and says: "Thanks a lot. Actually I was not able to handle it."

Anant replies with a smile: "it was my pleasure."

While he is about to continue the conversation, the bus he boards for his office daily, arrives and he have to leave. He steps out of shed to board the bus but it is still raining. He took his step back under the shed and offers his umbrella to her by saying:

"Hope you need this more than me."

She forwards her hand to take the umbrella but she is kind of speechless and shocked once again by Anant's behavior. She dint even knew how to respond to this but she takes the umbrella, with a smile on her face and says:

"Thanks."

Anant hardly listed her reply, he ran into the bus as he can't miss this bus. As soon as he stepped in the bus the bus starts to move.

Her eyes are on the bus and as the bus made a fine distance she smiles and whispers to herself: "OH! He speaks."

It's a fresh day morning again, sun is well hidden behind the clouds, and the environment is friendly and cooler than usual last days. It rained yesterday the whole day and last night too. The morning faint breeze is adding to pleasant environment. Anant is on his daily routine to the bus stop but today he left his room a bit early so he could be a bit slow on the way to bus stop and enjoy the morning breeze.

Anant is moving slowly with small steps on the pedestrian, paying no heed to the path ahead, his mind is absent from thoughts of tasks he have to finish today, instead he is relishing the chirping of birds who are sitting on the trees, trees which are planted on the sides of pedestrian.

He looks towards the left of Pedestrian and find birds drinking water from the scoops on the road where rain water is collected. A gust of wind blows sprinkling the water drops on him from the tree. Water sprinkling from the trees reminds Anant of his childhood days when he use to shake the small trees after rain to enjoy the sprinkle. He is enjoying the morning and this is eminent from his smile.

Anant is just few meters from the bus-stop and he saw her standing at the bus stop. Red skirt and white top with long earrings make her face more attractive and pretty. He went and stood next to her. After few seconds passed in silence, the girl notices him standing next to her and she says:

"Hey! Hi, thanks for the umbrella yesterday." while handing over the umbrella back to Anant.

He took the umbrella, and says: "well it's my pleasure, and I am sorry for the behavior the other day, was carried by thoughts and all."

And the conversation builds: "No issues, but after that I had a feeling that you are dumb,"

Anant narrowed his eyes with a smile, but she continued after looking at Anant's change of expressions, by changing the tone to more polite: "but that was proved negative yesterday."

Anant accompanied the statement with a giggle: "ok...ok."

"So what makes you late, today to bus stop?" She asked.

Anant could not find the humor in the statement and neither in the tone, but considering her week in making ironical statements he himself replied with humor and flirt:

"Actually, from yesterday I was thinking of you, so thought to spend some time with you, so here I am here, late." he ended the statement with a smile, breaking the eye contact.

"okei...y," she said, by deliberately blinking her eyes, taking it as a compliment. She continues, "but for that you need not to miss your bus, I believe?"

Anant again failed to recognize any humor, he looks at his watch it is showing 9:20, the time he left his flat, the rest picture is clear to him now. Actually he got up at 8:30, by the sound of alarm from his mobile, got brushed up from tip to top and looked for time in his wrist watch, which was showing 9:20, he found himself ten minutes early, than usual. The air was breathtaking which Anant could feel at his flat, which is only flat at the terrace of an old four story building.

His flat consists of a small room without any hall, a small kitchen, with hardly space for two people to stand at same time and washroom. The only pleasure he had at this flat is that, his flat is alone at the terrace and the roof is all his and the neighbor building could hardly managed to reach this height, so his building is the Empire State of the locality. And he leaves at the topmost flat of Empire State.

Anant could feel the free flowing cool wind at his flat, he thought to get on road for bus stop early, so that he could enjoy the weather. Anant left for the bus stop from his flat ten minutes early as per his wrist watch. He moved slowly and his steps were small on the way to the bus stop and he did enjoyed the morning breeze, birds chirpings and the sprinkles from the trees, but now it seems that the game is other way round.

Anant takes out his mobile phone from his trouser pocket and sees at what time he is running, he updates his brain with eighteen passed ten, and he is luckily out of luck this time. Not too many people do get this benign unlucky. He knows the next bus is twenty two minutes from now and he is late.

She saw the change of expressions on Anant's face, and she knows the bus number of bus that Anant usually boards. And besides that she knows the route of that bus too. She says:

"Well we have been talking for a while, but don't know each other's name."

Extending her hand she continued:

"I am Adhilisha, and I do work as a fashion designer."

Anant shakes the hand softly and replies to, so called an unasked question, but which should be answered, as our social ethics says.

"I am Anant, and have started a small business recently."

"That sounds as if someone is going to be rich soon." Adhilisha, says with a smile.

This sentence made Anant to blush, as if someone had spoken his heart.

Adhilisha continues:

"and designer house which is located in Hauz Khas, provides me a cab for drop in and drop out. And I will like if you will accompany me today."

Anant bewildered by the behavior of Adhilisha, the basic question raised in his head is that, how is she aware that his office is located in Hauz Khas.

"now you would like to appreciate how I know where your office is, well I saw you going in the same bus in which I use to travel before my designer house provided me with cab, so I know its route."

This is soothing for Anant, and he says:

"Yes! It would be a pleasure to accompany you, and seriously I appreciate your observation."

A white color cab came and Adhilisha and Anant both made themselves comfortable and it moved and so did their conversation.

3

Freaks

*I*ts eleventh standard class room, at the first floor, in main administration building of Kendriya Vidyalaya school. Winters have arrived and temperature is near to eight degree centigrade, the fog is very thick and even after the best endeavor of sun, its rays could not reach the earth.

Not even ten minutes have passed of second lecture, and the words of English teacher, Mr. Chadha, are hardly ringing the bell in the ears of Anant, who is sitting at third bench of the corner row, on the chair right next to window.

Anant's eyes are looking out of window, from which the view of football ground is clear and that of canteen too. The canteen is like a hive, which is always surrounded by students and most feavoured place for young couples. It's neither the football, canteen or the girls around there, Anant is that interested in. But, it's half visible basketball court hidden by another building of school, blurred by the distance and fog, on diagonal far end of football ground, is his apple of eye. His eye never misses any movement on the basketball court. He is looking directly on the basketball court ignoring what is happening in football ground or at the canteen and rather class for time being.

The corner window chair was not that easily to get, it's a hard earned chair by Anant. When the academic year was started children use to come early to occupy their favorite seat. And the definition of favorite for few children was the front seat so that they could pay more attention towards studies, for few others, favorite was the chair next to their crush or the closest possible they could manage, for those children who were always in a mood to enjoy every second of their school life and hardly gives a shit to what is going in the class, for them last benches were always in the demand.

The completion for chairs was stiff and those who use to be early use to get their favorite seat and as the days passed the seats were kind of labeled with the student. But all these were not the reasons for Anant to be early in the class during the early days of academic year and unlikely all, he wanted, not in demand 'a window seat.' Anant have a liking for nature more than other young kids who are attracted more towards the new fashion magazines and happening events, he like to sit at the window seat and enjoy the fresh air, from the window and he could see the basketball court and outer world whenever his class gets bore for him, and his best friend Rohit accompanied him by occupying next chair to him.

Well! The window chair was not that favored by the students of the class at the start of academic year but now it is one of the most favorite. Ritika the prettiest among all the girls of the class, have crush on Anant and is sitting right behind of Anant, the closest she could manage to sit, the next chair to her is occupied by Mansi her best friend.

It's not only the students of this class but almost half of the school had a crush on Ritika, not only from senior students but she receives the compliments from the kids in primary classes too. The very last day during the lunch when four of them Anant, Ritika, Mansi and Rohit, were on the stroll after having their tiffin's, a small kid of fifth class ran to her and said:

"Didi, would you play the role of an angle in our play, on annual day meet."

Ritika replied, in a soft voice:

"You should ask someone from your class, there should many girls in your class, aren't there?"

The kid replied:

"There are, but you are more beautiful than all of them, and angles are most beautiful."

so is she and her beauty famous in the school.

Now because of Ritika, the chairs around her became the most favored.

Winter days are on, students are wearing blazers and mostly all the windows are closed. But not the one at which Anant is sitting. He is still looking at the basketball court. Mr. Chadha was ignoring him for last few minutes, but it's been too long Anant is not paying attention, so he called Anant's name, but Anant is so busy in admiring the court and planning about the basketball tournament, which is scheduled in near future that he did not even noticed anyone is calling him.

Rohit first moved the book on the desk so that it may caught Anant's eye, but of no use Anant is deep in his thoughts, then Rohit pulled his elbow in Anant slightly and whispered his name, but this too is not enough to break Anant's focus, then suddenly a well swigged foot came from back and hit Anant's leg, Anant felt the pain in his leg, he turns back and with surprise and anger expressions mixed on his face he whispers to Ritika:

"What's the matter?"

"Anant Dixit" the loud voice came from front of the class. Ritika replies to Anant: "he is the matter" by moving her neck towards Mr. Chadha.

While turning towards the front Anant says:

"Yes sir"

The teacher said: "I suppose you are to stand, when a teacher is talking to you."

Anant rose from his seat and the teacher continued in a bit annoyed and angry voice:

"Are you there in class Mr. Anant?" stressing on Anant so that it sound more like a taunt.

And obvious reply from Anant:

"Yes sir."

"Well! Your behavior seriously contradicts it, I had called your name more than hundred times by now and you dint paid any heed."

"Sorry sir" replied Anant.

"I don't need your sorry, son. By the way, would you like to tell us what are we studying today?"

Anant's eyes made a quick scan of the blackboard, he could find 'THE ODE' written in center of the board, and it does not need a special brain to conclude that this is what is being taught in the class. So he replied the same.

The teacher knew that this would be coming, but he is sure his next question would make the battle one sided.

"That shows that you were attentive in the class." replied Mr. Chadha.

This sentence helped Anant to get his nerves control. And he collars it with a nod.

Then came the Yorker from the teacher, "So Anant, read from next line from where we left." fast and direct into the block hole and Anant is cleaned bowled.

Anant took Rohit's book from his desk and acted as if he knew from where to continue. Anant is sure Rohit would have been following the teacher and would whisper the stanza and the line number, as they have done this many a times before. But this time things appear to be different, Rohit too did not know from where to continue. Few seconds passes and Anant is standing pale, he slowly whispers Rohit's name. Rohit looks at Anant; Anant widens his eyes and indicates towards the book by tilt of his neck.

Mr. Chadha is looking at Anant, and as he thought he found that Anant did not had a track of what is happening in the class. He again asked Anant to continue reading from where the class had left. Ritika whispers from back, third stanza second line, but Anant did not got that. She spoke again but this too in vain.

Mr. Chadha waited for few more seconds and finally said: "You would like to leave the class, now."

Anant left Rohit's book on the desk and start to move on the way out, while he did not even made to the door, Rohit rose and asks the teacher:

"Sir can I borrow Anant's book for this class, somehow I forgot mine at home."

Mr. Chadha is quite irritated by Anant's behavior and on top of that Rohit's question sounds more irritating, the teacher replies in anger:

"NO, but you will accompany Anant outside."

This statement made Anant to smile, who had reached the door, and zygomaticus of Rohit also showed life. Ritika knew what all this is going. Rohit deliberately did this so he could accompany his best friend. Ritika whispers to Manshi in surprise:

"Don't you think these two are dick?"

Manshi gave her approval by a smile.

Rohit too with his head down leaves the class room. And Mr. Chadha continues with the class.

After few minutes Ritika's eyes caught something outside the window, which Anant left open, she got the glimpse of two boys crossing the football ground and heading towards the basketball court. And she murmured:

"Holly shit! These two will never change."

Anant and Rohit instead of standing out of class were going towards the basketball court, and they were easily noticed, as they both were the only ones crossing the football ground. Ritika is worried if Mr. Chadha sees them, then it could be trouble for them.

Anant and Rohit reached the basketball court and Ritika is relaxed as Anant and Rohit have faded by fog and more over out of sight, well covered with another school building. Both Anant and Rohit are wearing their blazers and oxford style black leather shoes, a perfect outfit meant not to play basketball, indeed any sport in that sense. But they are freaks like most of the school going kids, to whom dress hardly make a difference, both of them removes their blazers and places them behind the basket pole, folds their shirt sleeves, now they are feeling cold but they knew that in few minutes their body will get warm.

Rohit with the basketball in his control is practicing layups, and Anant is defending, it's almost few minutes for them in the court and their body temperature had increased, and sweat drops are sparkling on the face of Rohit, and he is breathing heavily. Anant too is sweating but cool and cram in his temper and focused, waiting for Rohit to make his move, so that he could react accordingly. Rohit on the drive took Anant with the surprise by giving a fake towards the right and crosses Anant from left, ending in a smooth shoot. Anant says:

"That was too quick and neat, we are improving, but still I fear we are not still ready for the Sports Day matches."

Actually, from one month now there is an Annual day celebration in their school, all track and sports events will begin one week prior to it and finals will be on Annual day. Last year they had lost in finals from D.P.S and Anant do not want that to happen again this year.

Rohit loses his tie, pulls up the sleeves of his shirt from his shoulder and wipes sweat from his forehead to make him more comfortable. He took a deep breath and replies:

"You know brother, we are the best team on the court, it's not more than a week we had won the finals in D.P.S., three tournaments in a row are ours, we have proved the best this year, and who knows this better than you captain."

"It's not I am denying our performance, but don't you think we are too proud of our achievements, and less focused on our practice" said Anant.

"I know Anant that we are not regular in practice, but the team players need rest and need to focus on their studies too. Don't worry brother just trust my words, all this was possible and will be possible in future because of two people."

"and who are they?" Anant interpreting in between,

"It's you and of course me, we will turn everything our way."

Rohit passes the basketball to Anant and says: "Now it's your turn to offence and mine to defend." And they both begin again.

4

Road to Home

Clouds are not empting their stomach now and neither are they making their presence felt by bright and loud lightning. This is first time since Anant Dixit had left Srinagar for Shimla clouds have become silent, but clouds have not yet left and neither faded, they could be seen anywhere and everywhere around, along the road, below in the valley and even above with the mountains. Anant Dixit who still had yet not reached Shimla is rowing his car through the smoke of clouds.

The art done by clouds could be seen all round, valleys, trees, roads and anything that is visible through the smoke of cloud, seems to be painted in snow white. In his journey to Shimla Anant had hardly seen any traffic since he had left Srinagar, the journey is about to end as Shimla is not that far now and neither traffic is accepted ahead.

The speed of a fine moving car with no traffic to accompany and none is accepted ahead suddenly is killed with the instant breaks on a U-turn along the mountain, leaving two dark lines on the road covered with few centimeters of fresh snow. The sound of breaks applied caught the eye of people who are standing on the valley side of the road. The opposing force of breaks is so strong that it threw Anant's head and back towards the wind shield and when the car stops he hit the driver seat again.

And finally he breaks words after four hours,

"What the fuck, is all this?" looking ahead to a long traffic jam. The traffic jam extends till his eyes can manage to see through clouds and in dim moon light. He releases the seat belt, makes him comfortable on the seat and tries to look as far as he can to find how long the jam is. He can only manage to see few vehicles ahead even after his best try, but he can see endless chain of fog lights in front, by which he can conclude that traffic jam is too long.

Anant turns towards his mobile which is placed on the side seat, plugged to charger with the hope of some good news. But in vain, he founds the mobile fully charged, but no calls and neither a message which he was accepting. One thing even in the odds for him is that his mobile is showing some network strength, which is almost like to discover a pile of gold accidently on a morning walk as he was almost out of network in his journey, and his cell is saying that it's five in the morning.

Anant unplugs charger from the mobile, picks it and opens the contact directory. Searches for a contact and he is looking at the mobile screen, he wants to call but something inside is holding him back from calling, his throat get chocked and eyes grew more red, a tear from the left eye makes its way down, he wipes the tears, takes a deep breath and places his mobile on the side seat.

Anant place his head in his hands in such a way that his palms touching his eyes and figures on his forehead. Anant is feeling the heat radiated from his burning red eyes, as the temperature of his palms is raised. Although Anant had placed his mobile aside but he is still thinking that: 'at least I should call once' but another part of him pulls him back and says to him that he need to be strong, all this will pass soon. Anant again took a deep breath and raises his head from his hands.

Anant looks at the window, which is fully covered with mist, light could hardly make its way through window glass, and Anant cannot have a good look of surroundings. Anant drops the window glass and looks outside, the cold moist wind makes its way inside the car, and passes through his face making him feel relieved from the tension that he is carrying in his head.

The warmth created by the car heaters is lost in few seconds, because of cold wind.

Anant could see a valley on the other side of road and few people from the vehicles that are lined ahead standing there. The opposite lane of road is clear, without any traffic, usually this kind of things don't happen in India, whenever a traffic jam occurs people moves to opposite lane too, which further adds to jam.

Anant is quite impressed by seeing people following the traffic rules and he knows, this is not because of people are following the traffic rules but there will another reason for this, which had forced them to follow the rules. A sound make to his ears coming from road ahead, a soft voice which is saying "chai, chai" that someone is selling tea.

Anant turns towards the road ahead and saw a kid of somewhat 10-12 of age selling tea, to the passengers in vehicles ahead. The kid is moving from vehicle to vehicle towards Anant, asking for tea. Anant's eyes got freeze on that kid, he knew he needs that caffeine, not only because he had not slept the whole night and he is feeling drowsy, but also he needs that to make his brain to work.

As that kid moves towards Anant, the effect of clouds and fog gets reduced and Anant could see the kid more clearly. The temperature is near to four degree Celsius or even below and the kid is just wearing a white colored sweater which is almost gray at places, designed with stains of tea and torn form right shoulder to chest, hardly providing him any warmth in this climate. The kid is carrying a kettle filled with tea, the handle of kettle is on his forearm, as the kettle is heavy for him to carry in his hand, and he is carrying paper cups in his another hand.

The kid moves more close, and he is just two vehicles away his voice is clear and Anant could hear soft words from his mouth:

"Saabh chai" the kid says while knocking the window of the car. The window came down and he gave them tea and after collecting his money and placing them in his trouser, he moves closer to Anant again.

The kid offers the tea to the individuals in the vehicle ahead of Anant's, but they dint pay heed towards him. Anant is watching every single movement closely, it seems the tension of what so ever he was carrying with him, is lost somewhere.

The kid reaches to Anant's window and says:

"saabh chai"

Anant hardly got his words as he is busy in looking at him shivering because of cold. The kid again asks Anant but this time in a louder voice: "saabh chai"

Anant who is almost leaning out of his window looking at the kid's shivering lean body, hears the words from the kid and approves with the nod that he needs tea, but says to the kid that he had lost his wallet on the way at Amritsar, where someone picked his wallet, so he don't had money to pay him. The road from Srinagar to Shimla passes through Amritsar.

The kid looks at him with a wired expression and to his dark colored BMW X3 (F25) too, in no way to him Anant is looking in a condition that he could not pay ten rupees for a cup of tea. But when the kid notices Anant closely he saw he too is shivering like him, the kid asks Anant that, weather he have a glass or cup. Anant replies positive and fumbles for mug on back seat of his car. Anant hands a well-crafted mug to the kid, which he purchased from Srinagar the other day when he was in Srinagar. While handing the mug Anant asks the name of the kid, and the kid replies 'Rohit.' The name is familiar to Anant, as his best friends name is Rohit too.

Rohit takes the mug from Anant, looks at the work done on the Mug, and again he feels other wise to the statement of Anant that he doesn't have money to pay for tea. But Rohit being a kid of road had seen worst accidents, tragedies, mishaps and what not happening on the road, and besides all this he can see Anant shivering and with eyes red, so he made a conclusion about Anant and starts to pour tea in the mug.

The mug is still not full and Rohit still pouring tea in the mug with his head down and eyes on the mug, Anant asks him:

"How long this traffic jam extends and what is cause of this jam?"

Rohit with his eyebrows raised looks at Anant for a glance and continues with the pouring, he hands the mug to Anant and says:

"Bhaiya, drink this first, you need it, you are shivering, and you may catch cold soon."

"Am I shivering?" said Anant and looks at himself, he suddenly feels the freezing cold, he feels the blood freezing in his veins and he starts to shiver suddenly with more intensity.

It is almost twenty minutes Anant had not looked at his cell and the pressure he was carrying is not showing any effect on him.

He finally says:

"Yes, I am shivering"

And a smile ran through his face and murmured,

"Limbic, my competitor, you awake again, I thought you were dead, for a while."

The kid asked,

"What!" who did not understood the murmur of Anant.

Taking his eyes away from the kid towards the mobile on another seat, Anant replies "nothing, I just remembered of someone."

Actually all this came from Anant's biology class, where he learned that, limbic is the part of brain, which makes you feel things which are not good for you, so that you can find a way to protect yourself or defend yourself. His limbic is active now, which is making him feel the cold so that he could protect his body from cold, and with cold it made him feel few other things too.

Anant is stunned with the behavior of the kid, that he is concerned about the health of someone whom he had never met before and besides the kid himself don't have proper clothes to wear and rather money to purchase them, he had given tea to that stranger for free.

Anant turns around toward back seat of his car after getting disappointed from his mobile and picks blanket and jacket. After turning forward he replies to Rohit:

"Thank you, I seriously needed this tea"

And hands the blanket to kid and continues:

"And you need this, more than money."

Rohit took the blanket and immediately put his kettle on the ground and wraps the blanket around him and says:

"It is too soft, is it made of goat."

Anant smiles and replies: "I don't know." and continue while wearing the jacket "can you tell me, how far this traffic jam exists and what caused it."

After picking up the kettle from the ground, in order to prevent the tea from getting cold because of contact from the cold road, Rohit briefs Anant and he lists all carefully while taking sips of tea. Rohit told him that the reason of road jam is that, near about five kilometers from here a land slide had occurred which had torn the road almost completely and Police is making efforts to keep the opposite lane clear from traffic so that when the road is prepared the vehicles from opposite side could move easily. And after this the kid moves ahead to sell tea, to those vehicles, who had recently lined behind, Anant's car.

But Anant is running with luck on this, his destination is Shimla and a turn approx. three km from here will take him to Shimla, but the problem is how to drive three kilometers from here, when the lane is totally packed.

Anant closes the window and slowly drinks the tea. There are two ways to deal with this problem he figured, which are pretty obvious to listen, first is to stay with the traffic and wait for traffic to clear, but by this way his problem does not resolve and for the traffic to get clear it would take too long. Second way is to take opposite lane and make his way three kilometers and turn towards Shimla.

Second way to deal the problem seems good and Anant chooses to work on that. But police is active on opposite lane, with the aim to keep it clear from vehicles, so that when landslide problem is cleared the traffic could move without problem. So the solution is clear, bribe the police and drive the way ahead, this is how it works in this part of world. But the problem in this plan is that here are too many police men on duty on the road, it is easy to bribe one but all. Anant may need a different hammer to hit.

Anant finishes the tea and thinks for a while before he moves out of his car. After hours of driving almost the whole night he is out under the sky, actually under the clouds. Immediately after coming out of car he stretches his hands wide sideways then twists his back on both side and stretches his legs at last. Anant locks the car doors and crosses the road. He can feel cold breeze making the way in his jacket, he buttoned it and closes his hands against his chest.

Standing at the valley side of road with his hands closed against his chest Anant takes a look at surroundings. The fog is dense so his eyes could not see a collect much from surroundings. He saw a valley covered with snow, but his eyes could not make till the end of valley because of fog. But a long chain of yellow fog lights of vehicles are comfortably visible. At a distance on road Anant could see a light, which he assumed to be a home of someone, the light appears to be hanging in air as the pole or wall to which it is connected is not visible because of dense fog.

Anant saw a police man making rounds. Most probably he is making sure that the opposite lane is clear from any vehicle. Anant went close to the policeman, and asks him about the reason of traffic jam, besides he knew the reason but that is the most obvious question he figured out to start with. While the policeman is telling him the reason Anant offers him a cigarette, in such a freezing cold and on overnight duty, it is somewhat impossible for the policeman to deny the offer, definitely a good move from Anant. And it happened as accepted, the policeman is taking few drags of cigarette, Anant come up with the question:

"Who is the officer in command here?"

The policeman finished the cigarette in four to five drags, and replies:

"Inspector Abhay Gautam, he is sitting under that red light" indicating with hand, at the same light which Anant noticed to be hanging in the air. The work of Anant is done, and now he knew what he needs to do. He offers another cigarette to policeman and came back to his car. He took something from his car and places it in his left pocket of jeans, and starts moving towards that red light.

As the distance narrowed the picture got cleared and the hanging red light slowly took the shape of tea soap, highly crowded by travelers. When he reaches, he saw two policemen sitting on chair on other side of crowd, he went to them and after sometime he took out his wallet from his left pocket of jeans and hands few thousand rupees to them, Anant shook hands and is on the way to his BMW. When he is on his way he heard the walky-talky of one policeman he crossed through:

"a black color BMW, is permitted to take opposite lane, due to casualty in it, that needed to be taken to ho..........."

And the voice fade, as Anant continues moving.

After reaching his car he make himself comfortable on driving seat, wears the seat belt, burns the engine and take a slight reverse and then changes the track, and then vanishes in the fog.

5

A new World

The sky is full of clouds, and the rays of the sun are too soft on the earth, but the rays were burning the earth since morning. It was a burning noon and evening again, it hardly appears that it rained the last day and almost the whole night. The pleasant environment of the morning was changed to hot and humid, as soon as sun took over in the noon. But now as the clouds mark their presence in the sky again, the fresh and cool air is making its way in the Anant's office, limbering down the temperature.

Anant's office is a simple two room office on the first floor. The outer room, which opens at the corridor of first floor, is acting office, the inner room which is bigger than outer room and acts as the godown. The way to inner room is through outer room. The first room is painted in white, a black wood table with four chairs is placed to the right of entrance of the room, the furniture of the room also include black wood chest which is full of account books, mostly new and untouched, and business plan papers. The table is occupied by an old computer and a telephone. The inner room is over following with cartons full of sports goods, stacked one over another.

It is the eight in the evening, almost all the offices are closed on the ground floor and the view of first floor is no different, except that of Unite Sports, which is still open. Anant is at work stacking the cartons of cricket balls in the godown, which surely is not a delight, as the cartons are not that light as they seems to be.

Twenty cartons already arranged in four different stacks, such that each stack contains five cartons. Last five cartons are to be stack, Anant who had placed a carton over another, goes for another carton. He grab it in his arms and is about to place it above the two carton stack, suddenly he felt the pain at his lower back. He stack it above two cartons, the pain not too severe but enough to make him stand with his hands on his back. Anant looks at the left cartons, and found that still two cartons left to stack. Anant murmured, while catching his breath:

"ohh! Last two to go."

Almost practically drowned in sweat, he grabs the next carton. As he raises carton higher to place it above the first three, the pain in his back rises too, and when he is almost about to place the carton above the three, the pain rises to such a level that it becomes difficult to bear it. But he could not place it at the top, so he bends slightly to comfort his back and when he is about to give up and place the carton back on the floor, a not accepted melodious voice break in his ears:

"Oks! You nest here, noo......t bad."

Anant recognize this voice, and the voice painted a smile on Anant's face. How could Anant forget it, he was listening her for more than an hour in morning on the way to his office, and recalled it throughout day whenever his brain was at rest. Now Anant collected all his strength and used it all in once to place the carton on the top. After placing the carton on the top and spoke while turning back:

"It seems someone is sniffing on me."

"Dear, unluckily you are not that attractive." She ended this with a smile.

"Well! That's really disappointing for me, you are truly a heartbreaker. Now god could only save me." Ended with a sad look, but his eyes ingesting her as much they can, and he ignored the pain in his back and acting like it was never there.

She made herself comfortable on the chair and placed her carry bag on the table, of Anant's office:

"Oh! I am a heartbreaker; I would rather take it as a compliment," making a gesture like tossing her collars, besides she dint had collars in her deep blue color top. She added further:

"well I will not mind if you join me on the table." with an engendered proud in her voice, and a smile at the end.

And Anant could not deny invitation, he left the last two cartons on the ground and further he added while coming through his store room to the outside room:

"Oh! That would be an honor mam. My greatest dream, to share a table with you, is about to come true."

After he had occupied the seat, he continued:

"So what could I do for you mam."

"Actually there is something that is making rounds through my brains since morning and........,"

Anant interprets in between:

"Well, no need to mention dear, I know I am best and unique." Stretching unique such that it sounds like unikkeee, making him proudly comfortable on the chair.

"That's nice try, but again I am firm on my opinion, still you are not that attractive idiot, but I should confess you are sweet." With a smile.

This idiot from the mouth of Adhilisha sounded more sweet then anything to Anant, which he knows she dint meant it.

Adhilisha continued:

"Actually my office closed and I was waiting for the cab, I called the cab driver, he told it will take half an hour for him to be here, so I thought to bother you. And it dint took me labor to find your office, I dropped you and saw you taking stairs, and how high could anyone climb in this double story building. Well there are exceptions that 'best and unique' people like you may get a 'daring and innovative' idea to establish office on the roof." She ends up in laughter.

The kid like soft but loud laughter is spread in room as perfume in air. While she is laughing Anant could not take his eyes away from her, staring continuously at her with a smile on his face and his heart is feeling something undefined. He has a work, to be done in the store, but the world around him and its tensions vanished in front of him all he can see is Adhilisha and her pretty smile. Suddenly a new world is visible to him. A new and a happier world which he had started to build, with Adhilisha as a source of all happiness he could have further in his life.

Usually the roads of local market in Hauz Khas are jam packed and on the Saturday evening like this, one can compare the crowd on the road with herd of sheep. And the herd seems to move slowly, in a particular direction, but in this crowd which is about to ooze out of streets a Hero Honda Activa is making its way through the crowd, not with ease but it seems that the rider had gained pile of experience in riding through these packed streets.

The weather is cooled by the evening wind and presence of clouds in the sky, providing relief to Rohit, but the crowd is undoing the relief by raising the temperature by few degrees. The heat is showing no mercy on Rohit, and his Eccrine sweat glands working regress to sweat as fast as they could to keep his body temperature low. The glands are too laborious and they are working so hard that his white color shirt is totally drenched in sweat. The sweat is causing more discomfort than comfort; he is sweating so profoundly that he is hardly able to decide whether to ride the Activa or to wipe out sweat which is making its way to his eyes.

It's not only the heat, but adding on that the crowd too is his opponent for the time being and every single who does not listen his horn which he is blowing and does not provide him way, irritates him like hell.

Rohit has to finish his work fast as it is getting late and he had plans with Anant this evening. He is thinking that he have to speed up as Anant would have already arranged the cartons and have made place for new cartons in the godown, which Rohit have to pick from courier service, and drop them at their office. Well as per his knowledge Anant is making place for new cartons.

Yesterday was the big day for Anant and Rohit; they had signed a new and big contract, so they need more stuff in their ware house to meet the supply of contract. After completing their work at office, they both will celebrate tonight in the same way as they use to do in their childhood.

They both will leave together for basketball match against each other at a court near to Rohit's home on Rohit's Activa. It's been more than two months they had been on basketball court, as they were busy in establishing their newly established business. And after basketball match they will go to a restaurant for dinner, and the winner of the basketball match will pay, like old days. Cycles have changed into Activa, but they are still <u>brothers from heart.</u>

Rohit killed the engine of his scooty in front of a courier shop and in the flash of seconds he is inside the shop, with keys still in his Activa, shouting:

"Pathan Shab, Pathan Shab, Pathan ...."

As he did not saw anyone in the courier office.

A big man of height more than six feet's and an big belly, appeared at metal stairs, making his way down, his size is so big that it seems these stairs may collapse anytime. While climbing down he said:

"Maya chilla chilla key kaynat kyun sir pe utaha rahe hai. Aapka saman bhahar rakhwa deya ta pahle hi, Anant bhai ka phone aaya ta."

Rohit smiled and give him a hug and said:

"Shukriya."

He left the office took two cartons and placed them at place between his legs in Activa, and dropped an SMS on the Anant's cell:

'received the stuff, on the way back'.

—————⊗⊗⊗—————

It's been more than half an hour, Anant and Adhilisha are still talking at unite sports office, and still they have a lot of topics to talk in their cannon. They seems to have known each other for too long no one could make it out from their talks that they had formally meat this morning and this is their second meeting. The whole floor is filled with their talks and loud laughter, their laughter is so loud that anyone can hear that clearly as soon as one reaches the floor. Adhilisha came up with something, she began:

"I was thinking ......"

And Anant's mobile beeped, he took his mobile and saw the SMS from Rohit, and replied to him:

"come fast bro, we got a lot to finish ☐"

After replying to the SMS, Anant looked back to Adhilisha. She stopped when Anant got indulged with his mobile. Looking back to her he said: "sorry, sorry please continue it was business."

"No worries you can continue, with that."

"I am done with it, we can continue." said Anant with the smile.

She resumed: "Actually I was thinking something, since yesterday about you."

"Oh! Not again, I know I am heartbreaking handsome." Anant interrupted with a wink.

"As per me it is the biggest misconception that a human can have about oneself dear."

Anant replied with a sad down face smile, "now you are becoming a heartbreaking girl." and Adhilisha giggled and said:

"That sad look looks good on you." Making fun of Anant "And don't worry I am really good in breaking hearts. And would you stop interrupting and let me continue."

"Ya Ya, please carry on." said Anant.

Holding her breath she continued: "Well! I was thinking. As per you, what am I supposed to do with the umbrella yesterday? I mean, I was already totally wet by rain when you gave me the umbrella, and that time I was standing under the bus stop roof, where rain could not reach me. So what were you thinking while handing me over the umbrella?"

This question left Anant wordless. He dint thought like this while handing over the umbrella. He thought he should offer, so he did, no such deep analysis of requirement and need. But within few seconds he came up with an answer:

"actually I was to board the bus and that umbrella was of no use to me either, I knew I would not be needing it further, as bus stop is right front of this building, but I dint knew about you weather you will be needing it or not so I thought to hand over to ......"

While he is completing his sentence Adhilisha's mobile rang, she said:

"Excuse me"

and attended the call.

It was the car driver he had reached her office to pick her, she told him the address of Anant's office, and asked him to reach here. Their offices are not too far and it will take few minutes for the cab driver to cover the distance. The call ended and she said:

"Will you work here the whole night? Or accompany me on the way to your home, I have asked the cab driver to reach your office; he will reach here in minutes."

It's an invitation which Anant did not want to reject, but he had a work pending, and more than he had plans with his friend Rohit, who would be probably about to reach with the samples.

While Anant is thinking what to reply, few seconds passed and it looked to Adhilisha that she have to go alone, but she asked again:

"Would you accompany me? If you don't have any important work to be completed"

A decision is to be taken right at the instant, on one side he have work to be done and prepare for tomorrows shipment, on other side Adhilisha and her pretty smile making its one sided game and he took it:

"Ya, please give me a minute, let me wind this and close the shutter.

While Anant is busy in winding up the work in office so that he could leave with Adhilisha, Rohit have reached the parking lot in front of the office building. Rohit is in hurry as he wants to finish the work as soon as possible and leave with Anant for basketball and dinner. Rohit took the two cartons in his arms, they are heavy but he did not want to climb the steps again so he took them together and left the Activa behind but this time locked.

The cartons are too heavy, he is bending backward to balance the load and his back and hands are seriously not enjoying it. Once he thought to call Anant below to help him but didn't as he thought Anant too would have been too tired of arranging the cartons in the godown.

Rohit is climbing the stairs and his heart is about to beat out of his chest. He is breathing heavily with his mouth. The cartons are up till his chin, finally he covers the stairs and the first thing he saw in the corridor is, Anant and a girl coming towards him and shutter of shop, down. He is not just surprised, but dam surprised, not because Anant is leaving the shop, with pending work behind, and they had plans for tonight that too seems to have least hope now, well these things too surprised him and as Anant is not known for living his work incomplete behind. But the thing that surprised him most is that Anant is with a girl, not just girl but a beautiful, too beautiful girl and he had no idea about that.

Rohit's breath seems to be limbered down to normal and he murmured:

"Now I see a dark horse."

He starts walking again and Anant too had noticed him, Anant briefed her about Rohit as his business partner and best friend, when they were talking in the office. Anant and Rohit stops in front of each other and Anant introduce both of them to each other.

"So he is the one you were talking about most of the time."

Anant nodded his head in yes.

She forwarded her hand towards Rohit and said:

"It's nice to meet you; I wish I too had a friend like you."

But his hands are all occupied, he replied

"Sorry I am occupied and this stuff is too heavy, you both carry on, I have some pressing matter to deal in office, and it was nice to meet you Adhilisha, hope to catch you soon."

"Yaa, that was nice to meet you. Babbaye."

Rohit replied: "bye."

And they moved in their direction. An unusual behavior from Rohit and Anant knew the reason.

When they reached down, Adhilisha said:

"Your friend seems to be too workaholic."

"Yes he is," 'but now he is angry.' murmured Anant.

They both entered the cab which was waiting for them outside, the car got the wings. And Anant pulled out his mobile and text Rohit:

'Sry brother I'll be early to ofc tomorrow, and complete the work.'

Soon he got a reply saying:

'Im nt angry about dat idiot. U are seeing a grl nd u nvr tld me dat, besides we had a plan tonight."

Seeing a girl? Anant thought am I seeing a girl? No actually I am not, it's just she came from nowhere to my office and asked me to join her, which I did not want to but her smile stole the ground and I am here with her, canceling the plans with my friend cum brother even without telling him.

"What are you thinking?"

asked Adhilisha.

"Nothing, nothing special." he replied.

And Anant's mobile beeped again, another message:

'but she is a nice grl, say sry frm my side to her, ll join you both some other day, I ll finish the wrk. u enjoy bro.' Anant smiled after reading the SMS, and thought that 'yes she is a nice girl'.

And Adhilisha and Anant talked the whole way. They shared their contact number so that they can contact each other in morning, as she invited him to accompany her to office again in the next morning."

The cab dropped them both at bus stop and they shared greeting and moved towards their own flats.

6

Breaking Rules

*L*ast twenty minutes had passed on the basketball court and the temperature of Anant and Rohit had considerably increased. Both of them are breathing from mouth but no one is ready to give an advantage to another.

The bell rang, indicating the end of the lecture and beginning of new lecture. They left the ball in the center of the court, collected their blazers and left the court to attend the lecture.

But the strongest words ever spoken by someone will come into play soon:

'I would have been the best human if I would not have friends around.'

Anant and Rohit are crossing the football ground and heading towards the class after punishment given by English teacher, which they turned into their basketball practice session.

Anant says: "Its Thursday today." and looked towards Rohit who nodded his head in approval, and Anant with a smile down face, after a sad pause said: "its chemistry period."

And Rohit burst in laughter and took few steps forward, faster than Anant and turned towards him face to face. Now Rohit and Anant are face to face, Rohit is moving backward and Anant straight. Rohit said: "you girlfriend would be waiting for you in class."

Actually Anant did not have good hands in chemistry, and because of which the Chemistry teacher usually point him, and all the questions are fired to him and then followed by punishment. To make fun of Anant his friends few a times calls the chemistry teacher his girlfriend.

"And she would be busy in her organic chemistry, for her world starts and end at carbon. The world is made of carbon, you are made of carbon, I am made of carbon and every single thing we know is made of carbon." said Anant in an irritating and mimic voice of his chemistry teacher.

Then they both burst in laughter.

While they were busy in their conversation, a hand came on Rohit's shoulder from back. He turned back and found Ritika and Mansi, Rohit said looking back towards Anant: "It seems your girlfriend had not made to school brother, what kind of boyfriend are you, you should take care of her." all four of them busted in laugh.

"Well! His girlfriend is eagerly waiting for him in class, but we are not interested in joining her." said Mansi.

Rohit and Anant looked to each other amazed, they could not believe Ritika is bunking the class. They have tried almost everything in their bag to convince her to bunk in last one and half year, but all in vain. And now from nowhere the trick is done and she is on bunk.

"Are you guys tired, or afraid to face us in basketball court." said Ritika with a wink towards Anant.

Anant gave her a smile and so did Rohit, then they four moved to the basketball court. Rohit, Mansi form a team against Anant, Ritika.

Anant and Ritika wins and as per their rules the winning team gives the treat. After the match they four moves for lunch, lunch is from Anant and Ritika. They cross the school fence for lunch as they were not permitted to leave school. Breaking rules together binds friendship more tightly.

7

Home

$\mathcal{T}$he engine of BMW car is pulled down in a parking lot of a hotel. This is sixth time in his life Anant is on the soil of Shimla. The queen of hill stations is one of the most favored vacation spots in India, but Anant is not here for vacation, but business. At last the journey from Kashmir to Shimla comes to an end.

It is early five in the morning, instead in freezing morning. Anant pulls the hand break and lies back on his seat with his eyes closed. As he closes his eyes, disturbing thoughts drains into his brain. He immediately opens his eyes and rubs them.

Anant looks around from his car and founds everything covered with snow. The hotel building, road, trees and even the deck of his car is white with snow and the snow is still falling. Anant was not even one kilometer down on road after bribing the police when it started to snow. Now looking at the snow, he feels contented that the money he gave to bribe the police in exchange of the path to Shimla had paid off. If he would not have taken that decision at that time he would have been in the traffic till now and the snowfall would have blocked the opposite lane too, and he would not be having any way to escape from there.

Anant zipped his jacket, as he knew that the heaters which are keeping him warm in the car will not accompany him outside. He took his mobile from side seat, but there are no calls, messages and neither any message on social networking site. But network strength is over flowing, a rare site to watch as he was practically running out of network for most of the time, in his journey. While looking at the mobile he said:

"Baby I know you will not disturb me" with Pan-Am smile on his face.

Anant places his mobile in his jacket and opens the gate of his car. A hotel boy runs towards the car, and takes Anant's luggage. Anant steps out his car and he can feel cold, the jacket he is wearing is not enough to prevent him from minus two degree temperature. He hurries towards the main hotel building, and the hotel boy followed him with his luggage.

Anant enters the main building of the hotel, but there is no one on the reception. The hotel boy puts Anant luggage and occupies the reception desk, Anant asked him for a room on third floor with valley facing view.

The third is the highest floor in the building and Anant like heights

After making an entry in the records of hotel, the hotel boy takes the keys to room number 303, and then he picks the luggage again and says in the polite voice: "sir, please follow me I will guide you to your room."

After reaching the room number 303 the hotel boy opens the doors for Anant, Anant enters the room and the boy carries his luggage inside. The temperature of the room is soothing and warm; the room heaters were running in the room and Anant felt relaxed as he was freezing with the cold.

It is a nice single bed room flat with separate powder room, with a large hall and balcony. Anant enters his bed room to have a look at it, the bed is soft as feathers, and Anant removes his jacket and throws it on the bed, break his hands which got stiff because of travelling. Anant come to hall where the boy is standing, the boy asked: "sir where should I keep your luggage."

Anant replies: "its fine there." The boy asks, "is there anything else I could do for you sir."

Anant went close to him, took five hundred rupees from his pocket and handed to the boy as a tip. And said, "Please provide me a mug of hard coffee, and make sure no one disturbs me from here after."

Antarix Bhardwaj

The boy leaves the room and Anant makes his way towards the powder room. The hotel boy is back in a minute with the coffee mug, while Anant is still in powder room, he did not knocked before entering as Anant made it clear that he do not wanted to get disturb. The boy looks in the hall but his eyes do not find Anant, all he can see is a couch facing television, table in front of couch and Anant's bag. He enters and places the mug on the table and left the hall silently. And places A DND tag on the door outside.

Anant came out of powder room, wiping his face from the towel, when he reaches near to the couch he saw coffee mug on the table, caffeine exactly what he needed. He places the towel on the table, grabs the coffee mug, and then made him comfortable on the couch.

Anant takes the sip of coffee; it is hard, exactly as per his taste. While taking the sip of coffee Anant look at the window, the curtains of the French window are fast, and the view of the snow falling in the balcony is mesmerizing but Anant take off his eyes from the balcony and avoids it as he had avoided many things on the journey here.

Anant removes the sleepers which he had worn from the front of powder room, folded his legs sideways and gave life to television, but after few minutes when he gets tired of flipping the channels and founds nothing worthy to watch, he finally switches off the television. It seems television failed to kill the thoughts that were running in his brain.

Anant wears the sleepers again and move towards bedroom, takes the blanket from the bed and wraps it around him. With coffee mug in his hand and blanket wrapped around him, he moves towards the window. The nature is so beautiful here that no one can avoid it, Anant tried his best till now, but the beauty of Shimla had forced him to enjoy it.

Anant pushes the window outside to open in balcony, the window is made of pine wood, and the touch of the pine wood is soft and cold. He steps outside and stands at the edge under the falling snow. Anant is looking at the deep valley full with pine, oak and deodar trees. On other side of valley he could see houses, painted all in white by the nature.

After few minutes, Anant again is lost in his thoughts and worries. He takes a sip of coffee from the mug, which he is covering with his hand, to avoid snow in it. Few minutes have passed, the coffee turns cold, his ears and hands are almost frozen.

His thought process is broken by sound of his mobile, ringing at a distance, inside the room. A phone call, this is the thing he was waiting for too long and finally he got one. He moves inside, place coffee mug on the table front of couch. Then moves to bedroom where he takes his mobile from his jacket, it is his friend Rohit calling him. He receives the call, lies on the bed and continues with the talk.

8

Moon is cute and beautiful

*I*t is evening, sun is about to leave to his abode, and it's time for Anant and Rohit to leave for the day. Since morning Anant is giving Rohit continuous explanation for his early leaving yesterday, besides Rohit hardly asked for them. It was a fair, hectic and tiring day for them both so far; they had dispatched the samples to their new client and managed the store room. The whole day they were almost on their feet.

They are about to close for the day, but still paper work is left, they have to update their ledger and delivery book before closing for the day. So they divide the work, Rohit is taking care of ledger and Anant of the delivery book. It took them somewhat an hour to update the work done by them this day. "The paper work is always the hectic one for us." said Rohit rising from the table. He breaks his back and hands to release the tension developed in them and now they are looking forward to their homes and their after a good sleep, all that is needed after such a laborious day.

Anant too finished the work soon and they closed the office. They both are climbing down the steps, and someone is climbing the stairs up. They both are surprised to see Adhilisha here. Anant is more surprised to see her here, as she text him about ten minutes before:

'I am leaving for home, how long will it take for you to get free.'

And he replied to her:

'Wish you a happy journey, and it will take me an half an hour and so.'

And on the contrary Rohit had different thoughts for this, as per him Anant and Adhilisha were sharing their ride back to their home as they did while coming to office in the morning. Looking at her at the bottom of the stair case Rohit slightly hits his shoulder to Anant's and turns slightly towards Anant and whispered: "She is looking good and what were you saying the whole day, that you too are not even proper friends. But this seems to be contrary." Rohit looks back towards Adhilisha and waved his hand and said, "hei, hiii. It's please to see you again. You are looking great."

She replied, "Hi"

She greeted both of them, in the mean while Anant and Rohit have reached the bottom of stair case. Anant greeted her back with a kind of happiness: "Hiii, I thought that you would have left."

She replied: "I was planning to leave, but I am here now, actually I was planning something."

She took her eye contact away from Anant and looked towards Rohit and continued:

"Actually Anant told me in morning that you both had a plan to party yesterday, but due excess of workload the plan was dropped."

Rohit thought, 'ya, the plan was dropped but not because of work but because this idiot is attracted towards you and for the whole day he was telling me about you.'

"So I am here, let's party. I mean if you guys don't believe that I am intruding, can I ask you both to join you."

Rohit said, "No that's not an intrusion, instead we both will enjoy your company. But our party is usually different than that you would be imagining. If you think, you can bear with us; we would be honored by your presence."

"Actually Anant told me how do you both enjoy, and will be pleased to join you." said Adhilisha. And they three started moving towards the road.

Anant and Adhilisha are dropped by Adhilisha's cab at basketball court near Rohit's apartment, where Rohit is waiting for both of them as he had reached here early on his Activa. After dropping Anant and Adhilisha the cab leaves. Rohit is on the basketball court practicing, but as he saw them arrived he left the court to escort them to the basketball court.

"You smell like a pig." said Adhilisha. "Yup, I know that. And it's because I was working like a horse." replied Rohit.

They reach the basketball court and Anant asked Adhilisha: "Would you like to join us on the court?"

"I will rater prefer to watch a match."

Anant and Rohit enter the court, and the match begins. Anant is playing an eye catching game, after every point he score, he shouts loud to catch Adhilisha's attention. But he is running back in the score. Tyche seems not much a supporter of Anant today, as he finally lost.

"And the winner is tame less horse and a word of advice, don't go close to him, he reeks like a pig." shouted Adhilisha. Listening to his praise, Rohit bow a bit in front of Adhilisha and said while raising his head, "thank you for the appreciation."

"I am feeling too hungry, would you both come for some food." asked Adhilisha.

"You both leave for the restaurant, I will join you shortly. I got some cleaning to be done" said Anant.

Rohit and Adhilisha leave for the restaurant on foot and Anant climbs Activa.

Rohit and Adhilisha are sitting at restaurant and are waiting for Anant to join them. They already had placed the order and the food is ready to serve, but they have asked waiter to wait till Anant join them.

"Where had he gone and what cleaning he had to do at such late in night?" asked Adhilisha, the tone is complaining one, as she is feeling hungry.

"You will shortly come to know." replied Rohit.

And finally Anant enters; they both watched him entering the restaurant. Anant is wearing a different dress and looking clean and fresh. "Now you know, what he was cleaning." said Rohit.

Actually, after the match Anant left for Rohit's apartment to take bath and change, to get free from the odor he had gained while playing basketball.

After reaching the table Anant throws a deodorant can to Rohit and said, "You may need this."

"I need food more than this now." replied Rohit. Rohit called the waiter to serve the food.

———— ∞∞∞ ————

It is ten past midnight and they all three walk out of restaurant, with their belly full.

Rohit said: "I will be taking your leave now. And it was awesome time with you Adhilisha."

"I too will remember this eve with you guys." Replied Adhilisha.

Anant and Rohit gave each other a hug and they all are on their way to homes. Rohit said bye and moves on his foots towards his apartment. Anant and Adhilisha climb the Activa and are on the way their homes too. Anant is riding the Activa and Adhilisha is sitting behind him.

A dark night with no moon visible in the sky, it's not that it is no moon night but the clouds in the sky are dominating. They have turned a full moon night into a no moon night, because of presence of clouds and breeze the temperature have fallen considerably.

Adhilisha is wearing sleeveless yellow top and three fourth jeans, but this is not enough to escape from the cold wind. The cold wind is doing its job quite perfectly, she got goose bumps due to cold, she is looking for an alternative way to escape from the cold, snuggle and rubbing her hands to keep her warm are already malfunctioning.

She folded her hands and places her head on Anant's back. The breath rate of Anant is disturbed. The moon shows itself in sky, as the fast blowing wind flew cloud away. Looking at the moon she said:

"Don't you think the moon is cute and beautiful today?"

Anant is thinking that, 'yes it is, but it had hardly any chances against you dear.' But he hides his feelings and said:

"Yes it is."

"But in few hours, this light of moon will be lost and will be taken by harsh and hard Sun." said Adhilisha.

"It is bad but a necessary rule of nature, let's understand it like this, moon is like good days and sun is like bad days in our life. When day are good and beautiful for us we hardly work but instead we sit and admire the good days. As soon as good days are over and bad days come then only we discover our true potential, and achieve things. If sun would not have been harsh we would not have discover our potential to bear the

71

Antarix Bhardwaj

heat. So bad days are needed to discover our potential" said Anant.

"That's another way to look at things. But I don't want sun to dominate in my life. If given choice I will prefer soft moon, and will work in good days to avoid bad days. I don't want this moon to pass and sun overtakes in my life" said Adhilisha.

"Every good thing comes to end. When moon shine in the sky, he knows his time in the sky is limited and he will be followed by harsh sun. We can only pray for good things to stay forever in our life. We can lie to ourselves and give millions of reasons to support that lie but we all know the truth deep inside that good days will be over soon." said Anant.

Besides Anant too don't want moon to pass, at least this moon to pass and this journey to finish, but every good things need to come to an end. They both moved ahead towards their home, towards the end of this journey.

9

Could have stopped him

*T*he crowd is so loud that the dribble of basketball is hardly heard. And why they should not be? Its last minute of boy's semifinal match going between K.V and guest team from St. Merry School, and K.V. is leading with 65-48. The home crowd knew what so ever may happen in the match but the reality is not even a miracle can make them loose.

The crowd is cheering, shouting, yelling, hooting and what not. The noise made to Anant's ear but did not ringed the bell of his head, for him as if the sound of crowd did not existed, he is totally in the game. He knew his team is going to win but he hardly want to take that way, he just want to add as much points he can add to his team score as he could.

St. Merry School is charging with the ball, Anant went to defend the feeder, the feeder tried to make a swift move towards his left but in vain as Anant was ready for this, but the feeder passed the ball to another player standing at three pointer area. Rohit immediately hurried to stop the player from taking a shoot, the player tried to cross Rohit but Rohit stole the ball and as soon as Anant saw that, he dashed off towards the opponent's basket, and Rohit passed the ball to Anant, Anant collects the ball and convert the pass into basket with the layup. The crowd gets loud and indeed louder.

Last twenty seconds to go and scoreboard is shining brighter than sun with 67-48. The ball is with the opposition and they making another move, the crowd started with the countdown 20, 19, 18......... and Anant knew they are going to win, he stood firm in defense and shouts louder than crowd "let's make it 70."

He moved towards the feeder again and the feeder passed the ball to another player, but from nowhere Rohit comes into picture grabs the ball before it makes to its directed destination. Rohit ran with the ball, the countdown had reached to 4, 3,...... and Rohit stop at the three pointer line and shoot the ball. The bell rings which indicate the end of fourth quarter and game too, but the ball is still in air and it made its way through the basket, making a fuck sound.

Rohit turned back and shouted while looking at Anant and said "we made it 70, brother."

Anant shouts in pleasure and the crowd breaks in the court. Ritika is first one to reach Anant, and said:

"congratulations my captain" with her eyes in his. And the crowd fills in like water.

The birds have just made out of their nests, flowers about the blow and sunrays just made through the fog to add soft colors to the dark landscape.

The pleasure of another ten minutes sleep after the alarm yells with its throat out in the morning is undefined, and the degree of pleasure increases during winters. Anant chocked the alarm and snuggled under his knit with his knees near to his chest and drops back in the dreams world.

The alarm marks its presence again and Anant knew he had to get ready for school, besides that it's his basketball final match so he could not afford to get late. But what so ever the priorities may be but crave for next few minutes sleep can never be under estimated. Anant fumbled the clock, chocked it again and felled with his face down on the bed, but he knew he had to get ready. Anyone can make it out from his sigh his lazy movements that how much he had to fight to get up, but at last he is on his feet's as he knew he is getting late.

The announcement of final basketball match had been on loud speakers since last done five minutes. The loud speakers barked again: "the best two basketball team in the district, have made to the basketball court."

The crowd which had gathered around the basketball court roared, the supporters of both the host and guest are almost equal in number today, usually the host crowd use to under count the other teams supporters, but today the scene is different.

The loud speakers continued: "on one side we have last two years winners and this year too they had not lost any match yet, in red we have Delhi Public School." The crowd cheers on support for the team.

The loudspeakers continued again: "and they will face the host team which too has not lost any match yet, in black we have Kendra Vidhaleya." And the sound of crowd was louder than the speaker.

The referee enters the court and asks the captions of both teams to come forward, both the captions come forward and they shake hands. The game is about to begin, the opponent captain and Rohit are at the center of court for jump ball, to start the game. Rohit jumps higher than the D.P.S. captain passes the ball to Anant who is standing in opponent's court during the jump ball. Anant collects the ball and took the layup to convert the pass into basket, with in four seconds of start of game the host is leading with 2-0. The crowd is shouting Anant's name, and with this shoot he had become the player to score maximum number of baskets in the tournament, by crossing the Rohit in the race.

The last quarter of final match is in its last minutes. The score board is showing 45 points for K.V. and 44 for Delhi Public school. Anant had scored 18 and Rohit 15 points in this match, Anant is still the highest scorer in the tournament.

The ball is with the opponents as they proceed with the ball, Anant shouts to his team: "defense, defense, let's hold them for few more seconds."

All the team players are too active as they knew just few more seconds to go and they will be the champions. The D.P.S. team proceeds Anant is defending the feeder, and all the players are on one to one defense. The crowd starts the countdown ten, nine, eight,...... last few seconds and K.V. is going to be the champion.

The D.P.S team is passing the ball but not getting a chance to shoot for the basket. The ball comes to player to which Anant is defending, they both are looking into each other eyes, Anant's eyes focused on him, he tried to cross him but Anant is quick and alert to stop him. The captain of D.P.S. team ran behind the player with the ball, the player with the ball passes the ball to his captain. The supporters of K.V. are at four, three,........., but now immediately felt too silent the pressure on both the teams could be felt.

Anant immediately took a spin around the player, crossed him, takes a step towards the caption of D.P.S., jumps to block the view of ring and stop the Captain from attempting the shoot. And all this happens in a flash of second. But few a times the fast are you, the faster is your opponent. This second is enough for D.P.S captain to make himself in comfortable position to shoot.

Anant is still in air with his hands stretched in air towards the ball, which is still in the hands of D.P.S captain, who too is in the air. Anant's hand almost reaches the ball but the Captain of D.P.S. releases the ball. Anant missed it by less than half a centimeter. Anant is still in the air and moving towards the captain of D.P.S. And to protect himself from Anant the captain used his hands and pushed him. The balance of Anant is spoiled he fall on court with his right knee making contact first, and blood started to drain from his knee, to which he dint paid the attention, for the time, he turned his neck towards the ring.

The crowd went silent the eyes of both teams supporters is on the ball, except that of Ritika who is still with her half heart to see Anant bursting his knee with court. This count or miss will decide the champions, the K.V crowd who were behaving like champions already are silent like dead, and the supporters of D.P.S. who were on their seats till now are on their feet.

The ball is still in the air, these last few seconds which ball is taking to reach the basket, can be felt longer than minuets. Finally the ball reaches the basket and the shoot gets count. The face of score board changes to 45-46 and the bell rings loud, which marks the end of game. D.P.S. team and supporters cheers and shouting in joy.

The supports of D.P.S. ran inside the court, and Ritika ran towards Anant. She reaches to him, bends on knees and asked him: "Are you fine." All that came from Anant's mouth were: "I could have stopped him."

"Get up dear, Embrace the defeat this is what builds victory in future." said Ritika. He tries to get up but his knee pulled him back, and he could feel the intense pain. Ritika shouts and calls Rohit, who ran immediately. Rohit helps Anant to get on his feet and Anant puts his right arm around Rohit's shoulder and left around Ritika's, and they start to move from the court.

10

Not to bother god

*I*ts life less silence in Anant's flat at hotel, nothing is making to the ear drums except the sound of swift cold wind and its conversation with the curtains and table cloth. The wind is moving in, freely through the French window, the window which Anant left open in hurry to receive the call this morning.

The table cloth is restricted by the vase placed on it from getting wings. Anant is lying on the bed, with his belly down and hands spread wide, making a shape of pentagon if four limbs and head are joined.

The melodious silence is abruptly broken by the alarm tone of Anant's mobile. Anant reaches for his mobile, chocks its tone and is back in paradise of dreams. But the alarm is not in the mood to give up that easily, it is back, loud and disturbing after five minutes. Anant takes his mobile and cancels all the alarms in queue.

Again he is back to sleep and covers his face with pillow. He is feeling the cold, as the wind blowing inside had decreased the temperature enough to be felt. But Anant hardly pays attention towards it, as he is treating sleep as a priority.

It is 15:15 hours and quite a time have passed since Anant had killed the alarms; he had those alarms set for his meeting that is to take place at 16:00 hours. It will take minimum of 20 minutes for him to reach the decided venue on foot. As per the schedule he had planned, he is already late, and still he is sleeping.

A sudden gust of wind unleashes the table cloth from the control of vase and the table cloth flies with the wind. The vase which was controlling the table cloth till now falls on the ground. The contact of vase and ground makes a thud sound and vase breaks into pieces. The sound is loud enough to catch Anant's attention and break his sleep.

Anant sluggishly rise from the bed; sleep is still oozing out of his eyes. He takes his mobile and look at the time, 15:18 hours. He knows he is late as per his planned schedule. But he had a bigger concern than that; he still have not received the call for which he was waiting for the whole night. By now he should have understood that he will not be getting any call. But he still could not give upon hope, which says that "keep your trust on me, maybe I could make you smile."

Anant places his cell on bed and move towards hall where he sees a vase broken spread on the floor. The fine pieces of glass are spread in almost half of the hall. The temperature of the hall is colder than the bed room; Anant carefully moves towards the window to close it.

Anant is already late for the meeting, by now he should have left for the meeting, and adding to the delay the broken vase is making his movement slow in the hall. After closing the window, Anant moves to his bedroom from where he calls the room service and informs them about the broken vase. And immediately after the call he hurries towards the powder room.

Anant is brushing his teeth, and someone knocks the door, he knew its room service, he replies loud enough to be heard outside of powder room:

"Please come in, but be careful the glass is all over, you may get hurt."

The door opens and someone from room service enters the hall and replies to Anant:

"Thank you Sir for your concern, now I will take care of this glass."

Anant continues with his brush.

Anant comes out of powder room after brush and shave, with towel in his hands he enters the hall, where he founds clean floor, freshly wiped with water and obviously no glass on the floor. The same hotel boy from morning is standing with cleaning material and says to Anant:

"Sir I have picked the glass, it is in your trash, please use it with care, I'll send someone from room service as soon as I'll find someone, to replace it. I would have replaced it personally but I don't have keys to their stuff. If you want I can take the trash with me, but then there will no trash to use in your flat."

Anant nodes and replies: "its fine I can use this trash, but make it sure it is replaced as soon as possible."

The boy replies: "Sir I will make it sure. Is there anything else that I can do for you Sir?"

"That is enough for the mean while" Anant smiles and continues "but can you clear one of my doubt."

"Please sir, I will if I could" replies the boy.

"What I can conclude from your words is that, you are not from room service, but still you did all this cleaning." enquired Anant. Anant is quite impressed by the work of this boy, since Anant had checked in; this boy is taking care of everything luggage, reception and room service too.

But the hotel boy took it otherwise, and replies with his head down:

"I am sorry sir, I agree it's my mistake, I should not have disturbed you when you asked me that no one to disturb you. But I thought you have not eaten since morning so I dared to knock your door, just to ask that in case you need anything. When I entered, you said there is glass all over so I picked it as it may hurt anyone."

Anant could see the concern in his eyes, that he doesn't want this to be brought up to his manager, and neither Anant is going to bring this in notice to anyone, at least not in a wrong way. More ever he is impressed by the services of this boy.

Anant replies: "Don't worry I'll not complain to anyone."

These words are soothing for the boy and he raises his head, he felt a kind of relief. Anant can see a slight smile and relief on boy's face and he continues:

"But I called the room service, about ten minutes back and no one shown up yet."

"Sir actually, snow is falling since night and its intensity rose in morning, most of the roads are blocked, so hardly any staff have turned up. Snow fall had stopped just half an hour ago and the cleaning of roads is still not in process. It will take some time for road authority to get in action. The staff will turn up soon, if you have any problem regarding anything you can tell me, I'll try my best to resolve them" justification by the boy.

Well Anant can understand this, in such conditions the staff doesn't turn up and those who have to leave they leave as their timings of work are finished, leaving a settlement in hands of god. He had seen this boy early in the morning, which was night shift and now too he is available, it means he dint not left hotel and most probably not even slept the whole night and day too. But few like this boy stay to save the settlement, and does not bother god for things that they can do themselves.

It is 15:35 hours; Anant is late to leave for the meeting, he had to scale distance ahead, which will take minimum twenty minutes. And more ever Anant is still not dressed yet. He knows if anyone could help him is this boy, so Anant says:

"Actually brother, your last statement had caused a problem to me. I had a meeting to attend at 16:00 hours, and it will take me approx. twenty minutes from here to reach Mall road. Even after best of my speed I could not reach the Mall road in time from now. As you said the roads are blocked, so definitely it will going to take more than twenty minutes I suppose."

The boy replied instantly, "There is a shortcut from here to Mall road, which will take not more than five minutes, but for that you have to climb the mountain with fair good steep slope, the slope of mountain is not concern but snow. Snow would have made the path slippery and dangerous. It's not road but a foot path used by local people here and indeed really short path."

This is what precisely Anant wanted. The boy briefed Anant about the path and mean while Anant got dressed up; at last he put his clock on and left the room with the boy.

When Anant and the hotel boy made at the main entrance of the hotel, the boy pointed the figure at the mountain slope, and said "this is the way to mall road. When you reach the top take left and you will reach Mall road. And while climbing use a stick to support you it will prevent you from slipping." Anant nodded in response, the boy continued, "but be careful sir, it is risky." Anant said in response with a smile: "thank you and I'll be careful." And Anant moves towards the mountain.

The path told by the boy was really short but not that easy to cover, Anant's foot slipped more than twice, and the energy his legs had to put in to cover the distance was in excess. But as it is said: 'All is well, when it ends well.'

Anant finally reaches the Mall road and still three minutes to go for his meeting, but he is really tired; Anant could feel his heart in his chest. "I am getting old." He whispers to himself and after collecting his breathe he moves ahead for the meeting.

11

Time makes it Strong

*I*t's been more than a year since Anant had started his business and almost the same time that he and Adhilisha are friends. The handwork pays and the same is seen in the growth of Unite Sports, it is doing a good earning, even better than what Anant and Rohit had thought a year before when they started the business.

Before Anant had meat Adhilisha his life was only full of planning about, how to make his newly stared business, a success. But since he had meat Adhilisha, he has few colors added to his life. They both travel together while coming to and going from office in cab provided to Adhilisha by designer house to her. They share their experiences of the days, plans of tomorrow and almost everything on the way.

A year is enough time to know each other, and they both almost know each other inside out. They celebrate each other's happiness and share each other's problems together.

Since two hours Anant and Rohit are in Maruti car showroom to purchase a car for Anant. Finally after two hours of selection procedure and paperwork they leave the showroom with a brand new Eon. It is not among the luxurious cars but he can only afford this for the time being, and more ever he is happy, it was in his short term goals to have a car and finally he have a car and finally he had it now.

Anant drops Rohit to the office and directly goes to the designer house where Adhilisha work. He had not told Adhilisha about that he is going to purchase the car. Actually he too did not knew that he is going to purchase a car today, it all happen in a flash, Unite Sports got an payment from a customer today and Rohit asked Anant to accompany him for shopping.

Rohit took Anant to the showroom and said: "I have two lakh in my account besides in companies account rest you have to arrange. Today we are purchasing a car for you." Flash and unpredictable this is what Rohit is few a times, as Rohit knew that Anant needs a car so he helped him getting it.

Anant enters the designer house and finds Adhilisha right on the front with a needle and stitching material with her; she is working on a white color wedding gown. Anant moves closer to her, but her attention is not diverted from her work, he stands right behind her but then too she did not noticed anyone behind her.

Few minutes passed and Anant is still standing behind her unnoticed, but he is enjoying watching Adhilisha. Suddenly she turns back may be for something that she needs to continue her work on the gown and she notices Anant standing behind her. Before she could ask him about how long is he standing here, Anant said, "Are you busy?"

"No, not much." she replied.

"That's exactly I wanted to here, so let's go out I got something to show you."

Adhilisha asks for few minutes from him to wind her work and asks him to wait on the couch. After completing her work Adhilisha came and they both left the designer house.

"Where are we going?" asked Adhilisha on the way.

"To the parking lot" replies Anant.

She thought that he would be with Activa; hence they are going to the parking lot.

When they reach the parking of the building, Anant stops in front of his brand new car, and said: "do you like it?"

"You must be joking?" she said with an excitement in her voice, she looks at his face and finds no sigh that he is joking, "oh my god you are serious." She almost jumps out of happiness, "it's amazing" she shouts out of joy.

"So where are we going for the ride?" asked Adhilisha.

"Ride I thought we are going for a party" replied Anant, and happiness could be seen in his eyes. "And you are driving" he throws the keys to her.

Its 2:00 in night and Anant limbers down the engine of his car, in front of shop which is directly opposite to the gate of Public Park. Besides being drowned in two 60 ML tequila shots and three Patiala peg of malt scotch, he still is in wits and vigilant.

Anant and Adhilisha have made their way here from a club, where Adhilisha was neck to neck with Anant in drinks. But the only difference is that Anant is with his wits and Adhilisha without them. It was 1:00 in the night and the club was about to close but Adhilisha was not in the mood to leave the club. Anant convinced her with all the reasons he could, to leave the club but she was not listening to him. After few minutes of persuasion she got convinced to leave the club.

When they were on the way back to their home after the club, Adhilisha came up with the idea to spend some time under the sky. And Anant hardly goes against Adhilisha, so they are here with the aim to sit in the park and enjoy the night breeze.

It's a big Park gate, and bigger the board which displays 'NO PARKING'. And Anant will mind to bother traffic police for his new car. So instead of parking the car in front of Park gate he parks it in front shop opposite to the Park's gate.

Anant and Adhilisha are in the car, and before leaving the car Anant scans the area around for police. He could not find even a human, everyone is sleeping in their houses and these two manic are on the road to enjoy the night. Anant opens the gate and steps out; he moves round the car and opens the gate for Adhilisha. She steps out of car; Anant takes her hand and crosses the road. They reach the gate of the park, and are not surprised to find the gate chained with chains thicker than Anant's fest.

It seems that their plan to enjoy the night breeze at the park is spoiled. All public parks are closed by this time in Delhi. But it makes no sense to plan a visit to the public park at night, when you already know that you will find it close. But they seem to have different plans. While Anant is looking at the giant park gate, Adhilisha starts to move on the pavement built around the parks fence.

Anant is still busy in looking at the gate. Adhilisha took a pause after moving six steps and asks:

"Will you accompany me or shell I move?" she is drunk and anyone can make it out from her voice and accent.

Anant turns towards her and said: "I am coming." He took a glimpse of his car parked and run to join Adhilisha.

It's a moon less night and the street lights are designed to enlighten the streets, the park is almost pitching dark but the street is full of light and visibility.

"I think this is what we are looking for." said Adhilisha, with excitement and eagerness is seen on her face, pointing at the tree ahead on the side of pavement. Anant approves by saying, "ya, this will do the needful."

The tree is grown on the outer side of pavement towards the road. They both move towards the tree. They are planning to jump over the park fence by taking cover of tree, its dark night but street lights are adding visibility, so they need something to cover them when they jump the fence. But I the shadow of tree will provide them cover to cross the fence.

They reach under the dark shadow of tree, Anant holds her from her shoulders and made her stand as she is trembling on her feet, and then he turns around to see that, is there anyone watching them or not? As crossing the fence of park is a crime and adding to that they are drunk, if police will see them they could be in problem.

Anant turns around, after finding the area clean, and while he is turning he is saying: "Now we can climb the fen............" pauses as he did not find Adhilisha. She had already crossed the fence and is sitting in the park. Anant is surprise to find her there, he said in amazement: "You gota be killing Me." with his eyebrows raised.

He again turns around to make it double sure but this time it is quick, then immediately he climbs the fence and jumps in the park. He moves to her and sits next to her, with his hands sideways and legs stretching forward, he look towards her and asks: "Are you fine?"

She turns towards him, with a big smile on her face, leaning towards him she said, "You are there with me?" Anant smiles and shook his head in acceptance. She continued, "Then how could you think I could be bad?"

Anant smiles to her and took his gaze forward, he closes his eyes and could feel the pleasure of silence around him, the air is fresh and cooler than his face hence he could feel the air on his face, he inhales deep and breathe out slowly, he murmurs: "this is awesome."

Adhilisha is continuously looking at him, while he is feeling the pleasure of nature. 'He is strong, responsible and sweet'; these things are making rounds in her brain. Her eyes is caught by Anant's hand which is close to her, she feels like holding it but few a times the simple jobs become the most difficult if they are thought in excess.

She looks at Anant face and towards his hand and again towards his face, now she starts to move her hand towards Anant's, and her eyes on Anant's face. She slowly moves her hand towards his, with her eyes on Anant's face, the wind gains speed and her hairs are flying in air. She is about to hold Anant's hand and suddenly Anant opens his eyes and says: "thank you this place is really awesome."

And she pulls her hand back, and looks forward and said: "I am always correct." And they both smile. And she punches his arm and Anant opens his eyes in shock and she said: "why are you smiling stupid, have I cracked a joke." And they begin to talk.

12

A Visit

$\mathcal{A}$lmost frozen and lifeless legs are being dragged on the snow, struggling with his right knee Anant moves slowly but continuous. Anant is too richly dressed in his black clock and jeans, but highly under dressed to fight the cold. The moon had just made his appearance in the sky, and with his appearance the temperature had fallen a bit below than negative three degrees. As the dominance of moon will increase in time to come the temperature will drop further. And the way Anant is shivering in the cold he had to make to his cradle as fast as he can.

With the decrease in temperature, the circulation of blood in Anant's right knee is reducing, he was feeling an intense pain with every step he took but now he is not feeling the pain instead his leg is getting numb. This is worst that could happen to him, Anant also knows this is because of lack of blood in his leg. He should feel the pain as 'few a times pain makes you feel alive.'

Previously Anant was taking steps but now he is dragging his left foot in the snow, this had increased the time for which his leg remains in contract with snow.

Dragging himself ahead Anant look for any help he could manage for himself. At a distance on left side of the Road Anant saw a vacant bench, he start to pull him towards the bench. But before Anant could make to the bench, a young couple occupies the bench, but there is enough places left for Anant to make him comfortable on the bench.

Anant reaches to the bench and without disturbing the couple he sits on the bench. The hard wooden bench feels more comfortable than any couch in the world to him. Anant closes his eyes and takes deep breaths, which relaxes him.

After relaxing for few minutes Anant opens his eyes and bends to see his knee. He starts to rub his knee with his hands so that some heat is generated in it, but this hardly helping him. He came up with new solution and starts to bend his knee and expand it with the help of his hands, this bending and expending is showing results, Anant can feel the warmth and the pain too.

Anant stood from the bench and all he knows is that he should hurry towards the hotel and with every step he should bend his knee as much as he could to keep the flow of blood.

Anant dint thought things could get this worst before he left hotel for business meeting, temperature is so low that his body is freezing and his right knee is on revolt again. The knee which he got injured during the final basketball match, do causes some problem for him occasionally, but this time it is getting severe.

Anant's decision to take the long route back to hotel is proving worst. After the meeting Anant's work in Shimla was over and he had no other place to visit, no other people to meet, and neither could he leave for Delhi because the roads are heavy covered with snow and he is not sure about the progress of land slide on the road which he left behind last night. All these factors combined together and he came with the idea to take a longer route to hotel, as this would take him time to cover the distance and when he will reach the hotel, he would be tired to sleep in no time.

But actually this is not the whole story, he don't want to give his brain much time alone. As loneliness make you think more of that, what you don't want to. He had not seen his mobile for any notification or message since he left hotel, besides his mobile had vibrated many times, may be for ping on wtsapp, Facebook, SMS or may be something else, but he had been completely ignoring it. Somewhere he had started believing that he will not get a call, and by looking at mobile he will get disappointment, so to avoid disappointment he is ignoring his mobile.

Actually the picture of mall road is not that bad as it is presented so far, on the contrary presently it is most happening place in Shimla. If we could take few steps back and sit on the chair to have a look at the mall road, we could see: The Ridge and Mall road covered with snow more than six inches thick. The while light of moon is adding a slight spark to the snow. The electric wires, shops, fences, benches all are covered with snow. It looks that the queen of hills is dressed in white gown.

Its winters, its snow and more ever its Mall road of Shimla, a perfect place to be at, to enjoy, to eat and to roam. Tourists have moved to Shimla like swarm of bee towards their hive during evening.

The Mall road is full of tourists, dressed heavily and looks like bears. The road is full of laughter and sounds by people, playing and enjoying. The shops on the road are full of local crafts and eatables. Happiness and positive energy is spread all around, some tourists are making snowman from snow, few are throwing snow at each other, rest are just enjoying the walk. And somewhere in between the enjoying crowd, tensed and struggling Anant moves slowly.

A small kid of 6 years of age, dressed from head to toe in more than four layers of cloths, looking almost like a baby panda in his exterior white fur sweater, is playing with his mother. The kid is running here and there and laughing, his mother is also happy to see her kid playing and enjoying. The kid ran and clashes with the left leg of Anant. The kid is about to fell, Anant's reactions came into play and he immediately bends to grab the kid besides the growing pain in his right leg. Anant grabs the kid before he falls. The sign of pain is clear on Anant's face as his ligaments had to stretch more.

Mother ran to collect her child. Anant hands over the kid to kids' mother, while the kid is still laughing. The lady took kid in her arms and said with the smile:

"Thanku, so much, you are a great man." a normal comment that came of nowhere, but true words direct from the heart of a mother, for a guy who had save her kid from falling.

A sarcastic smile ran through Anant's face, he thinks:

'Great man, if I would have been such great then why all this is happening to me.'

He smiled wider and replies to the lady in polite voice:

"Thanku mam, but I am not great, your kid is great and brave, and look sees he is still laughing."

They exchanges smiles, and the lady with her kid moves in opposite direction, and Anant too resumes his journey. Now he is on lower road, and the lower road is overflowing with snow and with less or almost no people on road. Street lights mostly out of function, but the few which are working makes this road look so beautiful like no other road in world.

The layer of snow is so thick on lower road that, for every step which Anant takes ahead he is digging out his foot from the snow. Slowly but carefully he makes his way ahead. Suddenly a low but familiar sound catches Anant's conscious and as he is moving ahead the sound is building up. The sound of dribble of basketball to his ears is an absolute melody in this deep silence, and he is being pulled towards that sound like an ant towards sugar. Towards left from main road he sees a basketball court, basketball something Anant could not resist.

A cemented basketball court, fenced with metal net from all four sides, with a gate to enter or to leave the court. Anant move close to the basketball court and stands at the fence, Anant is quite surprised to see the court; it is all clean from snow. The court is as clean that it seems that snow had never fallen on the court. To get the court this clean, someone would have cleaned it more than twice. He murmured, with a smile:

"Nice job boys." as he knows the cleaning would definitely have been done by them and after a long time he feels he is in company of his own clan. It is bone freezing cold and at this cold someone who is interested in basketball, or someone too interested or any one crazy would not be out for play, but one needs to be maniac for this game to be out in these conditions

He holds the cage with his hands and watches the boys playing, laughing and enjoying. He could see the energy and strength in the young blood, which he experienced as a school going boy but he definitely misses it now. The boys are not playing a match, just normal shooting, dribbling and practice moves, one of them who seems to look be the dominating by personality, collects the ball, places it on ground and says: "its seven and time for coach to come, let's do some proper warm-up," and no one said anything but it is clear with their body language that they agree with him.

Boys start to jog around the court, while Anant is busy in admiring the craze in the boys, a hand from back came on his shoulder and a voice of a female broke into his ears saying:

"Would you like to join us captain"

and she walks in the court, while the boys are jogging. A pearl white beauty, so fair that one can easily see blood in her cheeks, a damsel beauty dressed in three layers of dress, with blazer outside, wearing sports track inside after that and warm inner which is not visible from outside. Not enough to fight the cold but she looks comfortable and active in them. She took the ball from the court and called the boys.

Anant is totally out of words, he is surprised, confused and more ever attracted. It took him few seconds to bounce back from what had just occurred. A stranger girl I mean a captivating beautiful stranger girl, appeared from nowhere and called him 'captain,' something filmy had occurred just now. He look at her again with best of his sight, he found her familiar. He asked himself:

'Is she Ritika?'

He looks at her once again and his eyes responded, 'Yes she is.'

She waves her hand, to call Anant inside the court, he responds with a smile, and moves with the uncomfortable gait towards the gate. Besides the pain he is trying his best to walk normal, but could not, the jerk in the right leg could not be avoided even after best of efforts. He enters the court and the kids who are standing around her made space for him, he moves ahead and stands next to Ritika. She introduced him to the kids as:

"It's a surprise for me and luck for you that the best basketball player whom I have seen with my eyes playing on the court, is with us today. Anant, you all would have heard of him many a times from me, is with us. All I know about basketball is all I have learned from him and that's why I could guide you. He is so quic........."

Another surprise for Anant, he is being introduced like a superstar. His heart is pounding with joy, that someone from his past remembers him and remember him like a legend. But all she said is more than he accepted from anyone. He interprets her in between and says:

"This is really amazing day for me, (pause, and he looks at Ritika) seriously I was never praised like Ritika is doing and neither I deserve so much of praise."

He turns to her and smiles. She was already looking at him, with the smile all over her. She whispered with the smile:

"Thank you for coming."

And Anant could make it from her lips, what she is saying. Anant's presence here is mere an accident, he could not make it out why she is saying thanks to him for coming, it seems that she was accepting him here. He smiles wider and nods, because that's all he could do.

One of the four kids says, "So let's play coach, and Anant will play with us." Anant's knee is not in good shape but he knows if he plays, the ligaments of knee will get heated up and he will be fine. Ritika says "yes, me and Anant one side and you four on another, let's see who is good in team work." The match begins and Anant struggles in the beginning, but as the game proceeds he is comfortable on the knee, the boys are kind of surprised with new moves of him and team work by which Anant and Ritika both are playing. The game ended with Anant and Ritika winning.

Anant is feeling a new kind of energy in his body now, blood is rushing through his veins and he can feel it. The cloths which were not sufficient to keep the cold away have turned over sufficient now and his knee was never better before. His mind is all washed from worries, and he is not thinking of any mobile call and neither forcing himself to avoid it.

'Sport is the best heeler', and can be seen in Anant's case. He is totally relaxed and no need to mention tired too.

Anant is practicing with the ball, while Ritika is at the gate of the metal cage. The gate is towards the other half of the basketball court where Anant is practicing. While she is talking to the boys and seeing off them, one of them says:

"Didi, Anant is more handsome than you use to tell."

She smiles in acceptance of his comment. It's been almost eight years since they meet last, Anant had changed into a handsome gentleman from a sweet boy and Ritika into a damsel beauty. The boys left and Ritika turns around towards Anant he is busy in basketball to get his moves correct. She stood back near the gate with her shoulder resting on the metal fence. She stood there for some time wearing a smile on her face and her eyes just wants to keep on feeling the pleasure of his presence. It's been eight years. She wants to get a good look of him.

She moves towards him with long and soft steps, like a baby sneaking on someone, Anant is unaware of her and is deep dived in practice. She came silently and steels the ball, Anant shouts:

"That's cheating I was not prepared for this."

Both of them are giggling and Ritika said:

"You mean I should attack opponents by warning them, I don't think that is intelligence, captain."

She moved for a layup shoot, and Anant takes his position, focuses his eyes on her and makes a move in order to stop her, and says:

"But sweetheart, the opponent should know that he have any competitor, so he could make them pay back."

And he jumps and tap the layup, the sound of Anant's hand smashing the ball is loud. Ritika collected the basketball again and says:

"But darling the ball is with me again, and I have chance again."

She took a shoot and it gets converted, she continued:

"So how is that, my captain?"

He bows with his hands spread to side, and says:

"I am flat, coach."

"Oh you may rise, please, that's something I can do every next second" says Ritika with a touch of naughtiness in her voice.

Ritika collects the ball, places it in center of the court and they both start to move out of court, talking to each other and laughing.

Anant and Ritika moves through the street to the main road on which Anant was travelling. For every step they have to pull their leg from snow and dig that into snow again and suddenly Ritika throws snow on Anant, and Anant replies in the same manner, after sometime when they gets tired of the play they slowly moves ahead, cracking jocks on each other and guffawing. It seems they were never parted for such a long period, still they know each other's likings and all. The road is silent and alone, but accompanied with their loud laughter.

As the time passes suddenly silence break into them from nowhere, now both are looking on the route ahead, it's been more than a few minute they had not spoken, but the silence is speaking between them. Anant thought to ask her that what she does for leaving here, a formal question indeed but at least this will kill the silence between them. He turns to her and opens his mouth but co incidentally Ritika too spoke at the same time. They burst in a small laugh, and Anant asks her to proceed, with the smile. Ritika says with a smile on her face,

"Thank you for coming, I knew you will pay a visit."

The smile made her look so pretty that it can even make heart of stones to beat, but paralyses that of Anant. Because he could recall her saying these words in the basketball court too. His presence at the basketball court was a coincidence, there were no intentions to visit Ritika, and instead he was not even aware that she is in Shimla. Actually the sound of basketball and his need to get warm pulled him to that place. He had no idea why is she saying thanks to him. But he is keeping smile on his face.

Ritika looks at him again and continues:

"Rahul told me that you are here, and most probably you will not make a visit, because you are too busy with your business work."

Now the book is open and he can understand what actually is going on. He smiled wide and said:

"Ya, ya, I was really busy in my work, but a good friend is always worth more than money." a lie spoken with full confidence.

But unluckily for Anant he do not knows that, Ritika and Rohit never lost contact, ever since they left school they are in contact. Rohit never told him about it, maybe he thought it would not be worth. Ritika also knew about Anant's last two trips to Shimla in last year. She knew, he dint meant what he said just now, because if 'a good friend would always worth more than money' to him, he would have made a visit in his last two trips too, but she did not brought this in his notice as she is happy that he is here.

"Now there will be no point in telling what I do and how I am, you would have been briefed by Rohit." said Anant with a smile. Who was surprised to know that Rohit and Ritika are in contact, and Rohit never came up with it.

She smiles and says: "No I would like to hear about you in your voice." with a wink.

13

A Plan

$\mathcal{A}$ soft slow and romantic song is playing in the office of Unite Sports. And Anant who is sitting on the couch, with his eyes close, is murmuring the song, his head moves with the rhythm of music. He is enjoying and feeling the music deep inside him. Rohit who is sitting on the table is noticing him, and is quite surprise to see Anant lost in music.

Unite Sports have grown like a miracle in the market in four years. They started with a two room shop on rent, out of which the inner room they used as godown and outer as office. But now in the outer room a receptionist named Lata sits and in the inner room Anant and Rohit runs their office. The inner room is so lavishly decorated by Adhilisha that it can be compete with the ambience of five star hotels. And for storing purpose they have purchased similar three shops next to this one. Now Anant owns BMW X3 (F25) and an expensive flat. Things have changed too quickly during these four years, but Anant and Rohit are together like color and sketch in a painting.

Rohit rises from his chair and move towards the music system to which Anant's mobile is connected, unplugs the mobile from the music system, music stops, and Anant opens his eyes and says: "what happen?"

"I think you have a work to be done in store." said Rohit. "ya ya ya, I forgot that." Anant raises, took his mobile from Rohit's hand, plug in the ear phones, resumes the music, leaves the room, Rohit follows him till the outer room, but Anant hardly noticed him following him as he is too deep lost in songs and dreams. Anant leaves through the main doors of the office. Rohit who stopped near Lata's desk said, while he watches Anant going and murmuring the song: "Don't you think he is behaving like lunatic?"

"Excuse me sir, did you said something to me?" said Lata, who was busy in her work.

"Yes, don't you think there is something wrong with Anant?" He replied, still his eyes at corridor from where Anant had just passed.

"He is in love sir and anyone can feel that." she ended with the smile.

A courier boy appears on the gate. He took a paper from his pocket and read: "Mr. Anant" and Rohit said:

"yes I am." He handed a ring case to Rohit; Rohit opens it and founds a beautiful diamond ring. "Is it fine sir?" asked courier boy. Rohit replied, "It is more than fine." The courier boy says, "Sir, can you sign here." And Rohit duplicates Anant's signature, the boy leaves, and Rohit moves in the inner room.

After few minutes passed Anant is back in the office but now talking on phone, all Rohit heard is 'Ya I will be there in half an hour.' and Anant disconnected the call. Searching the contacts in his mobile phone Anant said: "where are you courier" Rohit who is continuously watching him, took the Ring case from the desk and said, "Is this you are looking for?"

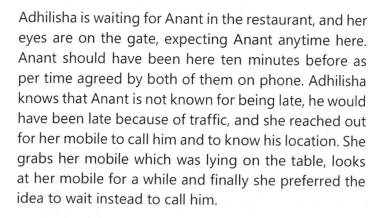

Adhilisha is waiting for Anant in the restaurant, and her eyes are on the gate, expecting Anant anytime here. Anant should have been here ten minutes before as per time agreed by both of them on phone. Adhilisha knows that Anant is not known for being late, he would have been late because of traffic, and she reached out for her mobile to call him and to know his location. She grabs her mobile which was lying on the table, looks at her mobile for a while and finally she preferred the idea to wait instead to call him.

Adhilisha is dressed in white, and look almost like a fairy in white. But when taken a closer look at her, anyone can see her eyes tensed and face down. It does not take any special skills to figure out that there is something not normal with her. She must be looking like a fairy in white but the energy around her is dark and negative.

Adhilisha see a black color BMW arrives in front of restaurant. The right door of the car opens and Anant steps out, with a bouquet in his hand, closes the door of the car and lock the car.

Anant is almost twenty minute late, late which he usually doesn't get. It's not traffic who is responsible for his delay but it's the bouquet in his hand. He took more than half an hour to decide which flowers to include in and what not to. Finally the bouquet in his hand is decorated with Juliet Roses, flame lilies and rarest of all ghost orchid.

When Anant reached the flower shop, the shopkeeper lady asked him what kind of bouquet he wants, he replied that he himself is not sure but all he wants is to make it special one. And when he was picking the flowers for the bouquet and excluded Gerberas and Margarita, the shopkeeper lady was also surprised and thought: 'he had excluded the prettiest flowers in the world and want to make the bouquet special.'

But finally when he came up with the flowers, and bouquet was build, the lady herself was impressed with his choices and she never had thought of such a combination. And when Anant took the bouquet and is about to leave the shop, the lady said with a smile on her face: "She must be too beautiful girl."

Anant who was sparking by looking at the bouquet turned to her and said: "She is the fairy and the best girl anyone could ever meet."

Adhilisha, who is waiting for Anant and with her eyes at the gate, is still with her eyes at the gate. Anant who has just locked his car behind moves to enter the restaurant and the guard opens the gate for him. Anant enter and finds Adhilisha in white sitting right in front, he said to himself: "I was wrong dear, even fairies don't holds the ground against you." With a smile on his face he moves straight to her. Her eyes are still at the gate, it look as if she is lost somewhere in her thoughts. She is silent from outside but she is fighting a battle in her mind.

"This is for you." said Anant after reaching Adhilisha. She is so lost in her thoughts that Anant took her by surprise. To cover her surprise she smiles but her smile is looking awkward on her and said: "Oh! You came, and thanks for this" while receiving the bouquet and continued "but there was no need for this."

This was not the reaction that was accepted by Anant. Adhilisha dint not want to hurt Anant but he had spent time to make this bouquet and more than time the bouquet was prepared with feeling, and Adhilisha's emotionless answer somewhere hurt him, but he decided to ignore it. She kept the bouquet on the table and said nothing further.

Anant check his pocket for the ring and after getting sure; he rests himself on the chair. "Thanks for coming."

said Adhilisha. "I was thinking to call you and in the mean while I was still thinking, my mobile started ring and it was you. It's been twelve days you were at your native place and we hardly talked properly, but I thought it will take you a bit more time to reach. I was planning to meet you at eve..." Anant get paused as his eyes fell on the luggage of Adhilisha on left side of her chair, he looked back to her, and continued "you directly came to meet me; you should have first gone your flat and took some rest. The journey would have been hectic"

"I thought we should need to talk first." She said with the pale and expressionless face. Anant put his hands on the table and leaned front towards her and said: "we are talking dear."

Adhilisha said "You are the best human I have ever meat in my life. And I" Anant interrupted in between and said with smile: "Well I know this, tell me something that I don't know." Old lines but few a times effective statement from Anant made Adhilisha smile too. "You look pretty dear." Anant said looking at her smile.

She recollected herself and with serious face again she began, "Promise me, that you will try to understand what I am about to say now." Anant nodded in acceptance. "I was at home and my parents want me to get married to Ashraf, when I told them about us, they strictly said no as you are not Muslim, I tried my best to convince them with what so ever I could, but they dint paid any heed to my reasons. Once I thought to leave everything and be with you, but then I thought of my younger sister and my family." she took a pause wiped her tears which ran through her eyes while she is speaking, "things are really complicated, I thought for days on this, tried to convince my parents about you and me, but no conclusion."

Adhilisha, who was looking down while she said all this, raised her head and look at Anant's face, which had turned pale and lifeless but she continues: "I know you love me nothing else I need from the world. You are only one whom I can ask to trust and understand Me." pause "Finally I accepted what my parents want me to do, you don't know how I am feeling, I am sorry Anant." And she busted in tears.

For Anant who is here to purpose Adhilisha for marriage, everything went upside down; he is almost broken into fragments, his heart is crying but eyes dry, face turned lifeless. He rises from his chair, picks Adhilisha's luggage, and takes a look at her, she is still crying. He wipes her tears, and with a forceful smile on his face he says slowly and softly: "Come let me drop you, to your flat." And he starts to move outside the restaurant with luggage and Adhilisha follows him.

The guard opens the gate and they both walk out of restaurant, Anant opens the back door and after placing the luggage on the back seat of the car he close the door. As he turns after closing the door, Adhilisha is standing right in front of him, and she hugs him and start crying on his shoulder. All she repeated in sobbing voice is, "I am sorry Anant, I am sorry ..."

Anant too holds her in his arms and said her, not to cry and things will be fine, while he himself is about to break in tears.

Anant opens the door of the car for Adhilisha, Adhilisha who is still crying enters the car and Anant closes the door, and he took a round of the car and occupies the driver seat. He ignites the engine and starts to move. Adhilisha is still sobbing. The head of Anant is numb, he doesn't know how to react and how to respond now, everything has turned upside down. Anant hands over the tissue papers from the dashboard of car to Adhilisha.

The engine of car comes to rest, in front of building in which Adhilisha rents a flat. It is twenty minute drive from the restaurant to Adhilisha's home but it took more than an hour for them to reach. Adhilisha comes out from car and is collecting her luggage from the back seat while Anant comes from behind and says: "I will take care of this." Adhilisha takes a step back and Anant took her luggage out. And they both start to move towards her room.

They took the lift and reaches to the Adhilisha's floor and then to her flat. Adhilisha unlocks the door and Anant hands over her luggage to her and says: "Bye dear take care." with a forceful smile on his face. Adhilisha looks in his eyes and embrace him and says: "I love you idiot." and she starts to cry again. Anant too embrace her in his arms and says with his throat chocked: "you are my life dear and I can't leave without you." And listening to this she tightens her grip around Anant.

After dropping Adhilisha at her flat, Anant moves towards his flat, on the way towards his flat he keeps the ring that he had bought for Adhilisha in the dashboard of the car.

After reaching his flat Anant take a look at his mobile and founds three miss calls from Adhilisha and two from Rohit. He drops a message to Rohit: 'bro, not in a condition to talk, will catch you soon.' And then switch off his mobile, as he needs time to think and don't need to get disturb by mobile.

After an hour of pondering over all worst things he can imagine and four beers running through his system, Anant comes up with an conclusion that, things are not that bad as they seems to be, all he need to be is normal and let things be as they are for the time being, but tomorrow he will meet Adhilisha and will talk to her about this and he is sure that she will drop the idea to marry someone else, as she too loves him. Then together they will find out a way to convince her parents and then things will be normal as they were.

Anant finishes his fifth beer. He tries to rise from the chaise to pee but his head is so heavy with thoughts and now drowned in beer too that he almost fall down but he prevents him from falling with the support of the wall and moves to the powder room and then with the support of wall he moves to his bed room.

The next morning like normal days Anant is waiting for Adhilisha in front of her building. He is thinking that they will leave for office together like old days and first of all she will be surprised to see him here as he did not responded to her calls yesterday. And once she came down he will treat her like an angel and then talk to her about her parents.

Almost half an hour had passed, and usual time at which Adhilisha leaves for office to have passed long back. He thought to contact her on her mobile but then he thought he should go to her flat and talk to her, as she may be almost broken because of all this.

Anant leaves his car and moves towards her flat, when he reaches her flat he knocks the door but no one answered the gate, he knocks for more than ten minutes but no response. Then he tries to reach her by mobile, but her mobile number is switched off.

The all positive thoughts that he collected over night and convinced himself to believe them have started to fade. His eyes are still red because of beer and tears in his eyes last night and once again he found himself helpless. He doesn't know what is going on now and how to respond to this situation. Then he controls his thoughts which are running wild now, by providing an explanation to himself again for her not being here, that Adhilisha would have left for office before he came and the explanation for her mobile switch off, that she would been too tensed because of the conditions and his behavior, so she would have forgot to charge her mobile.

Anant took the elevators and reaches the ground floor, where he looks for the building guard, who is not in his cabin. Anant waits for guard to return to his cabin as he thought that he would definitely have noticed her leaving for office, somewhere he still believes that she had not left for office, something different had happened which he don't want to accept. More than ten minutes passes and Anant is losing his patience, instead to wait for him he thought that it will be better to look for him.

In the garden which is in front of building, Anant saw a gardener, watering the plants. Anant goes close to him and asks him about the guard, the gardener looks up towards him and tells him that the guard is on leave for today, and then the gardener gets busy in his work again.

Anant starts to move towards his car, almost numb, all he is thinking is to visit Adhilisha's fashion house to meet her but this would not be a good time to make a visit, as she would be busy. So Anant plans to visit her during lunch hours. And moreover he is not sure that he will find her there or not.

Anant had almost crossed the garden, and is about to reach the car, a voice came from his back: "Shab, Shab, ..." somebody is shouting. Anant turns and finds that it's the same gardener, who is shouting and running towards him. Anant waited for him and when the gardener reaches, he confirmed that is his name Anant, and when Anant responded in positive. The gardener told him that a lady who leaves in the building gave a letter to him to forward it to Anant.

Listening to this heart rate of Anant had gain speed like nothing. He is thinking what would be in the letter? Why did she leave a letter? And what not. The gardener moves towards the guard desk and carries back a red envelope. Gardener hands over the letter to the Anant, pays his greetings and leave for his work at garden.

Anant is again surrounded with the thoughts that could not be defined but felt by Anant. He sits in his car and tried to limber his thoughts, after some time he removes the letter from the red envelope and opens the letter and reads:

Hi Anant,

I knew I should be telling you this face to face, I tried yesterday to call you many times but you dint received my calls and after some time your mobile was switched offed. You cannot understand the pain I am going through, I could not sleep for last three nights properly and all I want to do is run away with you somewhere where me and you and only be there. But when I think of my family the things get more difficult for me, my parents and sister, if I take a step to be with you this society will make their life worse.

My marriage is four months from now. I already find myself as a puppet without life just following the society rules. I may get married to anyone but my heart will be always yours and I pray to Allah that we will be together after this life. This path is too difficult for me to travel but when I think of you it becomes impossible. I request you one thing that please don't try to contact me in future, I will not be able to handle it. You are love of my life and I know you love me more than I could love you ever, but it's time to forget me.

Yours and only yours Adhilisha.

It is four in the evening. The doorbell is ringing since last ten minutes and no one had responded to door yet. Then Rohit took the key from his pocket and opens the door of Anant's apartment.

The hall of Anant's apartment is all meshed up things are lying on floor and vas broken, Rohit can make out what would have happen last night. Rohit enters the bedroom of Anant, and found Anant lying on the bed with his belly down. Anant's mobile phone lies on the floor, broken, near the malt scotch whiskey bottle, which is almost empty.

Rohit repeated tried to contact him on his mobile phone but was all in vain, Rohit had not talked to him since last evening when Anant left the office with the ring to purpose her for marriage. And the only type of communication that Rohit received from Anant since then was a message which said that he is not in the condition to talk. So finally Anant decided to make a visit to Anant's house and know what is going.

On the way to Anant apartment, Rohit was thinking that Adhilisha would have rejected the purpose or would have acted in the way Anant would have not accepted, that's why Anant is not responding to him. But this is normal for Rohit now he had seen them fighting on simple things in past, he knew that things will be fine between them soon. But the scene of Anant's apartment is beyond he accepted, thing are terribly bad and Rohit can sense it.

Rohit goes to the kitchen to get some water for himself and what he found is five beer bottles empty. Looking at the bottles he smiles and said: "he is too thirsty."

Rohit grabs the bottle of water from the Fridge and goes to the bedroom again and aligns Anant properly on the bed, start the air condition and leave the room closed behind to sit in the hall. Rohit have to clean the couch to make some space for him to sit and then he switch on the television.

Eleven in the night and finally Anant wakes from his bed. He opens the door of his bedroom and finds Rohit watching cartoons on the television. The noise of door caught Rohit's ears and he turns towards Anant. Anant greets him by saying hello. Anant knew Rohit is here because he did not turned to office today, so there is no point in asking and neither did him.

Rohit take a good look at Anant, Anant is still in the effect of liquor, his eyes are red and he is too lazy to walk. But Rohit do not want to talk anything about all this as he can guess what is only friend is going through. Rohit replied: "Hi, and finally the sleeping baby is up" and smiles wide and Anant smiles back, "you would like to take bath" continued Rohit.

"Ya, I need to take bath" replied Anant, and leaves to powder room to take bath.

After bath Anant comes and sits next to Rohit, and Rohit gives him a glass of water with disprine tablet dissolved in it. Anant smiled and took the glass and said: "stop being my mother. And thank you." And Rohit drink the whole glass of water.

Few minutes passes in silence and Rohit asked "What happened yesterday, you were to purpose Adhilisha for marriage."

"I didn't purpose her" replied Anant. The answer is quite surprising to Rohit.

"And the reason for this is?" asked Rohit.

Than Anant told him the whole story, Rohit was accepting that something had went wrong but he did not thought that things could have gone to this level. Rohit can see water in the eyes of Anant, which he had never seen in past. Now Rohit can understand the gravity of the situation, now he had to be more careful while talking to Anant as he don't know what could hurt him now.

Rohit didn't find any words by which he can help Anant so kept silent. Rohit is thinking how can he take Anant out of this apartment and make him meet some new people so that his brain gets a bit busy and he will think less of this. It is ten past two in the night and all the clubs and discs are closed. Closed, are they really closed, well as per law they are closed but when any government makes a law to stop anything they take source of income from many and few people gets a business opportunity, they start a business against the law and earn huge.

Rohit knew the place where they go on whole night. Rohit rises from the couch and says: "I have a place to visit would you accompany me." He did not said exactly what he is planning, as he knew if he will tell him that they are going to a place where it is illegal to be at this time of night and besides he is not in the condition and neither in the mood to go anywhere.

Rohit takes a turn in Silent Street, no one could be seen in the street but the cars, and Rohit drives his Audi slowly in the street. Anant is highly under dressed to be at any place except his home.

Looking at the empty street Anant asks: "where are we going?"

"You will soon come to know" replies Rohit.

Rohit parks his car on the side of the street, leaves the car and starts to move, Anant follows him. Anyone can make from the gait and face of Anant that he does not want to be here. But Anant knew that he should not be alone, as loneliness will arouse many thoughts which he don't want, so he is here without knowing, why he here for?

Rohit raises the shutter of parking of one house, the parking is empty, they enter the parking and Rohit closes the shutter again. Anant is following Rohit without any questions, as it hardly concerns to him that where are they going, he just want Adhilisha to be away from his brain and her thoughts too.

As they move ahead in the empty parking, a door appears. Rohit opens a door and a different world is visible. A lavish and noisy party in going, the crowd is among the rich families of Delhi. Anant had never been to party like this, besides liquor; herbs, drugs, chemicals and almost everything that is available in the world to make a human high is available in here. The music is loud and mostly people here are not listening music but feeling it.

Anant who is found of parties and night outs is accepted to enjoy or at least join the party. But Anant goes and sit at a corner. Anant is not here mentally, he is still thinking that what he can do to convince Adhilisha, besides he don't want to think of her and want to enjoy the party, but he could not pull the rains of his brain and control the horses of thoughts. The worst part to be in this situation is the more you force your brain not to think, the more it thinks.

The lights of the club which use to create ecstasy to Anant and the sound which use to pull him on the dance floor are all annoying him. After few minutes he leaves the party and tries to contact Adhilisha on her mobile phone but her mobile phone is still switched off, he knew that she had switched of the mobile but he can't hold himself to call her again and again.

Rohit come outside of party to see Anant, he founds Anant is with his mobile phone in his hand and is trying to call someone. He wait for few minutes and when

Anant gets tired of calling her and places his mobile in his pocket and then Rohit goes to him, and asked, "I am done here shell we move." Rohit can see that Anant is not enjoying being here and besides he is not comfortable to be here so Rohit decides to leave the place.

The next morning, Anant opens his eyes in Rohit's bedroom, he is not fully out of sleep but he snuggles for his mobile, something he is used to. Every day when he wakes up he searches for his mobile and founds a good morning message from Adhilisha, this is how the day begins for Anant. Few old habits do not go so easily, and this will too take time. After few seconds he releases that he had broken his mobile yesterday, when his body was over following with liquor and his brain with thoughts of Adhilisha.

He realizes that it's been almost twenty four hours and he had not tried to contact Adhilisha and what in case Adhilisha would have released that they should talk and tried to contact him, she would not have been able to do, as his mobile is broken. Immediately the shadow of sleep and laziness vanishes from him and he leaves the room and enters the hall.

In the hall he does not find Rohit but the landline phone, this is exactly he needs at the moment. Luckily besides his own contact number he memorizes Adhilisha's too. He dials her number but the hopes shatters immediately as the operator says that 'the number he is trying is switched off.'

But the hopes still leave and Anant leaves the apartment, catches a taxi and move towards Adhilisha's apartment. On the way he is thinking that once he will meet her, he will make things fine. But when he reaches to her apartment he founds that her apartment is closed. When he enquires from the guard and gardener he comes to know that she had not returned to her apartment since she left at evening of day before yesterday. On enquiring further he comes to know that when she left she was carrying two bags with her.

Now Anant knows that Adhilisha had most probably left for her native place permanently. Now he is left with no other choice to leave for his home or to office. He is still thinking that what went wrong that Adhilisha is acting in this way. At least she should have given him a chance, as he have a plan to make things fine. The plan Anant is thinking about, is to talk to Adhilisha's parents and convince them, but he don't know what will he talk and how will he convince then, but he is sure that he can convince them.

Anant want to give it a shot, he wants to meet Adhilisha and her parents and try to convince them with all he has. But Anant could not find a way to talk to Adhilisha or her parents. Now he is criticizing himself for not receiving Adhilisha call, but all that is past he has to look for a way to get in touch with Adhilisha now.

As it is said 'when you want a solution you get it and when you don't want you get an excuse.'

Anant thought for a while and now he has a way. Anant boards the cab and leaves. The cab comes to stay at Fashion house where Adhilisha works or use to work. As per him they surely would be having information about Adhilisha, as she would have informed them. Or at least they would be having her native place address, in their records.

But no one in the office knows where Adhilisha is, as she had not informed anyone in the office and they have address of her flat in Delhi but not of her native home.

Rohit is busy on phone with a client and Anant in ledger. The phase when Anant was so week that he was not able to hold himself and neither his emotions have passed. He had gone through the sleepless nights, crying and thinking what his mistake was and why Adhilisha didn't even gave him even a chance, and he had a plan which would have made things normal.

For more than a month he was not eating properly and was alone in his apartment. But Rohit was always with him, every day he uses to make a visit to Rohit and spend as much as time he could spend with Anant so that he could recover from Adhilisha.

Finally after three months, since this week Anant had started coming to office and resumed his participation in business.

The call with the client is over and Rohit turns towards Anant, and finds him busy in ledger. Rohit is happy to see his friend, his brother back and busy in work. He smiles and says to Anant: "Brother I have some work in godown; I will be back in some time" Anant node his head and Rohit leaves.

While Anant is still busy in ledger, his mobile rings, Anant is using the same old number but a new mobile, he looks at his mobile it is an unknown number. Anant receives the call and says "hello" and on the other side was the voice of a female and Anant recognize this voice.

After completing his work Rohit returns to office. As Rohit enters his eyes goes on Anant, Anant is sitting on the chair with his head in his hands, Rohit joins him on the chair next to him and asks him: "what happened?"

"Adhilisha called, it's her marriage a month later and she wants us to be there" replied Anant.

Rohit could hear the change in Anant's voice, Rohit asked him: "even after what she had done to you, do you still love her?"

"I can hate her, forget her, criticize her but the truth is, I cannot stop loving her" and while he is saying this his eyes gets filled with water and voice becomes heavy.

Rohit is left speechless by Anant's reply; he can understand what Anant is feeling now.

While sobbing Anant continues "these days I was thinking, if all this was to end like this, why did fate us brought us together?" pause "may be because god want me to suffer, or I have would have hurt too many people and I deserve this"

Rohit is still silent and could not collect the words he can say to ease his brother.

"you know Rohit few days before my eyes were full of water and I stood in front of mirror, and said that I will not cry in future, not because I am strong but I don't like them in my eyes."

Anant cleans his tears and smiles (forcefully) and speaks: "but like most of the things, these tears too are not in my hand they drain out when they feel like."

After holding himself and taking a deep breath Anant continues: "few months back I dint have her contact number and neither her address and I was dying to arrange them anyhow, now suddenly I have both but I don't have guts to meet her. Now I don't know how to face her. I can't meet her."

Anant stops and Rohit brings him a glass of water.

"I can't meet her and neither will I. I have a plan, I will not be here I will leave for a place far so that even if I want to meet her in future before her marriage, I will not be able to. I don't know how I will respond to when I will meet her, she wants us to be there at her marriage but I can't see her going with someone else." Anant again cleans his eyes.

"and for my life time I want to carry her image of a fairy in my heart and she will be my dream girl throughout my life, she can take her from me but she can't remove herself from my heart, even if she want to I will not let her. I have told her today that she may call me in future if she is ready to be with me, or don't call me ever."

Anant stands and leaves may be because he want to cry more and openly or he don't want Rohit to see him like this. Few a times tears should not be stopped they should be made to flow like uninterrupted river. They take stones which have settled in the heart with them and make flow of life smooth.

14

Time has come

$\mathcal{A}$nant had lost the track of path approx. half a mile before, where Ritika turned left from the main road they were walking on. Now the path is guided by Ritika.

Anant hardly knew where they are going to end up. But he is comfortable to walk in these streets as snow is less on them. It's been half an hour since they had left the court, Anant's muscles which were warm because of Basketball they played are getting cold and pain in his right knee is gaining strength, he is deliberately bending his knee more with every step they take so that it generates some warmth.

They take another turn towards left and the main road which was visible at rare behind is now not visible. Anant is trying his best to remember this route, few times the street had climbed up and few times it had fallen down, but this is the first time it turned towards left, and Anant is keeping track of every inch.

Anant wants to know where they are going, but he dint asked yet as he thought the destination would have be near and they would be reaching soon, and moreover it would look awkward to ask Ritika. But as pain in his knee is making its presence felt again, he is left with no other option but to ask. So he started with the formal and usual questions:

"So what do you do here in Shimla." asked Anant.

"I work with a bank, as a manager." replied Ritika.

"Ah.aa! You a bank manager, I am flat," paused Anant.

Ritika look at him with a smile and eyebrows high.

"seriously I am flat dear, I mean a manager with an athletic body, who would not want his account in your bank."

Ritika replies with the glitter of happiness in her eyes:

"You know what?"

"What?" replied Anant.

"You still are a dog."

Anant felt some vibration in his jeans he immediately pulls out his mobile. He founds Rohit SMS which says:

'how was the hunt, my killing man. I am sure u would have killed few.'

Rohit is asking about the meeting, and how many new clients Anant had convinced to work with them.

Anant replies to him: 'the hunt was ours and now the forest is our :p'

Anant types another SMS to Rohit: 'plz feed me with the update of marriage.'

He places the cell in his pocket and says: "sorry for the mobile." And they continued with the conversation.

It is Adhilisha's marriage today at 11:00 PM. And this business tour was deliberately planned by Anant as he doesn't want to be in Delhi during Adhilisha's marriage. He had hold himself with what so ever he had, from getting in contact with Adhilisha since that day Adhilisha called him and invited him to attend her marriage ceremony. He knew that he will not be able to hold himself on day of her marriage, and neither he will be able to see her getting married to someone else, but he don't want to create problem for Adhilisha and her family. So he planned for a tour, so that even if another side of him wants to do anything on this day he could not, as he will be far away.

One side of Anant says that he should have given a try and tried to hold Adhilisha back with him, when she called him a month ago and he will regret throughout his for not trying at all. But another side of him says that had done what was right, as there was no point in trying at that time, Adhilisha was with her mind set to follow her parents. But the truth is that he was, is and will be fighting with both sides throughout his life, as both the paths were right and at the same time both were wrong.

The thoughts of Adhilisha and her marriage are disturbing him, foe few days now he is waiting for Adhilisha's call but till now he dint received any. Now he just wants this night to pass so that he would not be left with any option to get close to Adhilisha.

So far he had done a great job and since he had played basketball and meat Ritika, hardly had he thought of Adhilisha till now, but his mobile interference had reignited the fire of thoughts.

Ritika looks at Anant and founds him not walking comfortably and lost somewhere, so she asks. "This is because of that final basketball match?"

Anant is lost in thoughts and her words dint reached to him, she repeats again but a bit louder this time. Anant looked at her and said "I am sorry, I was somewhere else, and can you please repeat that."

Ritika smiles to him and said: "dear you were not just somewhere but you were lost there. And I was asking that, your knee does not seem to be in a good shape, is it because of injury you got on that final basketball match?"

"Ya it is, sometimes in cold this knee gets in a mood." said Anant and ended with the smile.

"Don't worry dear it will not take much time. We are almost there." said Ritika.

But Anant did not even know that where they will be soon, so he asked "So manager, where are we going?"

"We are going to enjoy, 'the best tea' available in Shimla." Ritika said, stretching her right hand towards left in order to show direction, "this way" as they were turning "aa...nd we have reached." she said.

And they enter a small street which is almost clean from snow and beautiful embroidered with old architecture houses. Few may be of prior independence of India and lighting is heavy and eye-catching it seems like a piece of paradise is cut and placed here. Anant's eyes got alive and he whispered of amazement: "wooow". His eyes wide open and he is busy in watching the architecture all around, every house is better than another.

Few houses are made of wood and this is the finest architecture of wood Anant had ever seen his life, 'no wonder a tea in restaurant at such a place would be more worth than distance they had travelled.'

He asks: "So where is the restaurant" still with eyes on the wooden houses.

"Restaurant?" with the surprise, "did I say that we are going to restaurant?" said Ritika.

Anant did not know what to say, he was and is unaware of plans which Ritika is cooking. She took few steps ahead and unlocked a gate: "here we are, to my home where we will enjoy the best tea in Shimla." she said with a wink. These words spread the smile on Anant's face too, "it means besides being with the best curvaceous manager I am with the best chef too" he said with a smile.

They both enter the house. Its dim light inside, Ritika enlightens the house by pressing the switches, which are behind the gate. As the lights induce colors to the house, Anant's eyes took the scan of the whole house, it is not a big home, and he could see a square shape hall in front of him, not that lavish but the roof of the hall is royally carved and painted. Rest the house looks extremely simple and clean, with a couch placed in center of the hall and a 42" l.c.d. on the front wall to couch and house music system. A chest on the left side of hall which have trophies and shields that Ritika had won, few of them he recognize as they are from their school.

An open kitchen on the right side of hall and he could see a door, which he assumed to be a bedroom. Ritika shut the gate behind and crossed him and says: "welcome to my home, make yourself comfortable showing couch with her hands."

Anant moves forward and sits on the couch, and stretches his right leg straight. Ritika switches on the room heater and places the keys of the house on the chest, which was in her hand.

"Give me a minute and I'll be back." said Ritika. Anant turn around to look at Ritika, as he was busy with his knee, he looks at Ritika and smiles "sure" he replies.

Hardly sleeping since days and nights, and adding to that he is too tired because of basketball match, all these combine to make Anant feel drowsy as soon as he sits on couch.

The temperature of room is warmed by the room heaters. Anant had removed his shoes and is massaging his knee softly with his feasts. Ritika enter the hall from the room, she had changed to a more comfortable dress of pink color. She stretches her arm and offers the crape bandage and diclofenac gel to Anant, and said "hope you need these." Anant looks up at Ritika and accepts the bandage and gel, he replies with a smile.

Now she moves towards the kitchen and Anant's eyes at her, she got a charm, a lot different from the girls which Anant had met in the recent past. He could not get his eyes away from the curvaceous athletic figure. He closes his eyes took a deep breath and said, "You are looking ravishing. And the temperature of room is heating up because of your presence" she dint turned around but said "thanks".

15

Breakfast

*A*nant is taking turns on the couch, but there is hardly place for that on the couch finally settles on his stomach with his left hand hanging down from the couch to ground. But he could not hold this position for too long, finally after few minutes of struggle on couch he finally wakes up and sits on the couch. But he doesn't leave the blanket as it is warm and comfortable with it. He wraps the blanket around him and sits on couch hardly covering any place on it. The room heater is still burning but then too blanket has its own leverages.

Anant is surprised to find himself at Ritika's home. The last thing from last night he remembers is Ritika was preparing tea, they both were talking about the fun that they use to do at school and he was feeling sleepy and was yawning.

He looks around for Ritika but dint found her nearby, so he looks at the door behind where she went for changing last night, and brought bandage and diclofenac gel, thinking she would be sleeping in her room. But the door is closed, so he called her name few a times, so that she will respond by hearing it.

After two three attempts when Ritika did not responded, he concluded that that she is not in the house as he tried the highest pitch he can. He thought to contact her on her mobile, but he doesn't have contact number either.

But this thought has touched a different string, the night of Adhilisha's marriage had passed, and he has to look at his mobile for any updates from Rohit on Adhilisha's marriage. But the mobile phone is not in any of his pocket, he search the couch as mobile may have slipped out of his pocket during his sleep, but of no fruitful results.

His eyes still are not completely open, drowsiness still has full control over him. He looks at the ground with his squinting eyes for his mobile, but nothing is in the area his eyes could scan.

Anant bend further to search his mobile under the couch. Eureka, drowsy eyes finally found the mobile but it is scattered into parts near the leg of the couch. Luckily nothing is broken just disassembled so he picks the parts and assembles them. Now he is all set to go.

Anant wants to leave to his hotel room, to get daily ablutions, and leave for Delhi for his another business meeting to be held tomorrow. As the snow would have been cleared and roads would have been on move but before that he had to inform to Ritika that he is leaving.

He is pressing the power button of his mobile so that he could call Rohit, as he remembers that Rohit and Ritika were in contact, and from Rohit he could get Ritika's number, and could ask about Adhilisha marriage.

But the mobile is not getting switched on, may be because the battery of his mobile which was charged almost 36 hours ago in the car, could not have manage to last till now. Anant place the mobile on couch, as it is of hardly any use now.

Anant rose from the couch and it was effortlessly, his knee is so normal that he did not even felt anything abnormal, and it is so smooth that he dint even noticed that his knee is fine now. His knee is like normal days, the way it usually is. Anant is on his feet and breaks his body to shed the laziness, he moves to the chest and founds the house keys.

'Keys are here, and Ritika would not leave house without the keys,' he thought. But he could not found her near and neither had she responded to his voice. So he came up with the basic conclusion that, she must be sleeping in her bedroom.

He moves towards the bedroom door, and knocks the door slowly just once, so that if she is awake then only she could reply, as he don't want to disturb her in her sleep. And he did not receive any response from inside.

Just to make double sure that she is there, he opens the door slightly and peep inside, but contrarily to his belief she is not sleeping and neither in her room. He could see a bed with a crumple bed sheet on it, and a big teddy on the bed. Looking at the teddy he says: "No matter what, girls will be girls" and he smiles.

He saw an attached powder room on left side of the bed room. He knew he should not enter anyone's bedroom without the permission but he had hardly any choice.

Anant enters the bedroom and while he is moving towards the powder room, he could hear the sound of shower from the powder room. He reaches the door of powder room and knocked the gate, the showers stop and sound came from inside, "oh! You awake, give me some time I will be back. And I have prepared the tea and sandwiches; you can found them in kitchen." Anant replies, "Ok, I am waiting outside." And Anant could hear the sound of shower again.

Since last evening when Anant was at the business meeting, he had eaten nothing. Even at the meeting he got snacks to eat, not a proper food and before that he was sleeping the rest day, and on night prior to that he hardly ate anything, just chips and tea were satisfying his stomach.

Anant pours the tea in two cups from the flask, and took the sandwiches which Ritika had prepared to the table in front of couch, and again he is on couch. He is feeling too hungry and the smell of sandwiches had increased the hunger.

On the other side Anant want to go to his hotel so that he could pack and leave for Delhi, neither he cannot eat nor can leave; social etiquettes sometimes bind you from what you want to do. And Anant is facing the same situation.

Anant went to the music system which is placed below the LCD, so he had to bend on knees to operate it. He is choosing the disc which has music of his choice, in the meanwhile Ritika came out of her bedroom after taking the shower and saw Anant busy in selecting the music and two cup tea on the table accompanied with sandwiches, "The tea must had been cold by now." said Ritika. Anant looked over his shoulder towards her, "may be, but I have poured the cups hardly a minute before." He places his hand in the pocket of his jeans and took out his mobile phone and shows it to Ritika and says, "Do you have charger for this?"

She looks at the mobile phone and said "Apple?" Anant nodes in the affirmation, but she shows her Samsung mobile and said with her eyes squint: "We are enemies in this department." and they both laughed.

Then Ritika moves towards the kitchen, after taking the tea flask and two fresh cups, she came to sit on couch and placed the flask and cups on the table. As she knows the tea poured by Anant in the cups had went cold. Finally Anant found what he was probably looking for slow Bollywood songs.

After playing the songs on home sound system Anant joins Ritika on the couch, for breakfast. Ritika is looking at Anant, with the eye that he will ask her to excuse him so that at least he may go and clean his mouth. But this is not the first time Anant is going to have the breakfast without cleaning his mouth, so he is hardly paying any attention towards that.

But Ritika is looking at him, but he dint responded as Ritika thought. Anant looked at Ritika: "Is there anything we need to finish, or we waiting for someone." said Anant. "From my side all things are done, you must be having some unfinished business." replied Ritika, with a hope that he will remember to clean his mouth, if he had forgot. Anant smile in response and said: "No, no we can start with the food, and I am feeling too hungry."

Ritika pours the tea in fresh cups, and they begin with the food. Anant is so hungry that the normal potato sandwiches were like Grilled Peanut Butter and Jelly Sandwiches to him. During the breakfast Ritika told him about last night, that last night she was preparing tea for him, and in the meanwhile he slept. Ritika then brought the blanket from her room and covered him with that.

After the breakfast, they are washing their hands in the wash basin at the kitchen: "The breakfast was really yummy, I had not eaten such tasty sandwiches ever." said Anant. "Oh! Thank you. You can have them tomorrow too." Ritika said with a smile on her face.

"I wish I could, but I have to leave for Delhi today." said Anant. Ritika looks at him and says: "Ok, then you can wait for your next trip to Shimla."

"Ya sure, and I would like you to disturb me in Delhi whenever you make a visit." said Anant. And they both leave the kitchen together; Anant sits on couch and start wearing his shoes. After wearing his shoes he stood up, and says to Ritika, "It's time that I should leave for my hotel, from there I'll leave for Delhi."

He is almost ignoring the land slide that took place on the highway, because of which he had to bribe the police. It's been almost 36 hours when he was on that road, well a considerable time to clear the road and resume the traffic. But anything could happen when snow and hale are creating disturbance.

"I heard that there is landslide on the highway." said Ritika. "Yup, it's been more than 36 hours since landslide occurred, and I know road authorities are slow but I am sure 36 hours are enough to clean the road and resume the traffic."

Ritika is almost convinced from inside that the landslide is not clear, as she had been leaving here, and she knows that Anant is not leaving to Delhi nor today and neither tomorrow. But as he knows Anant, there is no point in convincing Anant that road would not be clear, as he would not believe till he himself make it clear. So she says: "wish you a happy journey, and if something makes you stay back in Shimla, you are welcome at basketball court at evening."

Anant leaves the house, and Ritika wave her hand standing at the gate. But the since last night he is more relaxed mentally, he had hardly thought of Adhilisha as his brain dint had time to think of anything except what was happening at that movement.

16

Another Day

*A*nant is on the way back to his hotel, the roads are almost clean from snow. Looking at the roads which were cleaned in a single night, Anant's hopes are high that the land slide would have been clear and he can leave for Delhi. But before that he is in hurry to reach his hotel, where he could charge is mobile and confirms the marriage of Adhilisha, but the eagerness to know about Adhilisha had considerably reduced since last day.

Anant is walking on the valley side of the mountain road, on one side he can see the clean but still low on grip road and on another a deep valley still covered with white blanket of snow. The road has come to life again; it is being travelled but carefully and slowly. And the valley which runs deep down is gorgeously decorated with snow. Anant is walking on the valley side of the road, besides being the wrong side of road to walk, now he just want to enjoy the nature, whereas he had missed all the scenic on the way to Shimla. Things are changing in him, and he can feel more life around him than in him.

Anant's hotel became visible, and he is walking slowly towards it. He stops on the opposite side of road in front of his hotel and stands with his face towards the valley. He could see the tall oak trees crowned with snow, deep valley full of snow, everything is frozen but still at peace. He closed his eyes, smokes out a deep breath, and says: "I will be back soon to meet you nature, if I would not have meeting at this evening at Delhi, I would not have left" He smiles and move towards the hotel.

Something from inside is stopping him from leaving this place, but as the work demands he have to leave without his will.

As soon as he enter the hotel premises, he looks at his car, which is well parked at the place where he left it, and it is been cleaned from snow, whereas most other cars did not received that treatment from the hotel staff. He moves to his car, opens the doors, grabs the charger from the dashboard, and starts to move towards the entrance of main building of the hotel after closing the door of his car.

Anant enters the main building of hotel, with an impressive, confident and straight gait, and with the same old attitude on his face. The gait is more than enough to catch the attention of two receptionists who were not there at night when he checked in and neither when he left for his meeting last day.

The receptionist watches him entering and now moving inside the hotel, as per there knowledge he must be a new guest to their hotel, but he is walking directly inside the hotel. Looking him not stopping for enquiry and making his way direct to main rooms, one of them stops him by saying, "excuse me sir, may I help you."

The taste of sandwiches made by Ritika is still on his tongue and he want to eat more of them and his stomach is not full either. He turns back to receptionist and says: "it would be really kind, if you will send some potato sandwiches to room number 303 and tea too." He turns back and is on the way back to his room.

The doors of room number 303 opens and Anant enters the room, the window is closed and the room temperature is warm, he removes his clock, plugs his mobile to get charge and moves to powder room to do daily ablutions.

Anant had just come from the powder room, wearing the gown. Someone at the door knocks, Anant says to come in. The same hotel boy came with the sandwiches and tea, places them on the table and says "Is that all you asked sir?" Anant nodded his head, in positive response.

The boy again asks, "Is there anything else I could do for you sir?" Anant sat on the couch and pours the tea in the cup and replies to the boy, "when I entered the hotel I say my car, and it was cleaned, was that you who did that."

"No sir it was not me, but I told the individual who looks the parking to do so." replied the boy.

"Is there any specific reason for this special treatment." enquired Anant. "Yesterday when I was leaving for home after long shift of work, and was standing at the entrance of building, I saw your car, it was covered with snow, I went to man in charge for parking and asked him clean the car, no specific or special reason for that, I just felt and asked him. I am sorry if my action offended you." the boy ended with his head down.

Anant, who is taking sips of tea, looks back to him and says: "No it's not like that, I just wanted to know so I asked. And one more thing I would like to ask is that, the landslide on highway is clear or not."

"The landslide that took a day before is cleared, but if you are going towards south, which I am sure you are going as your car number is from Delhi, you can't go."

Anant is already impressed by this boy's initiative taking quality but now he is killing with his observation skills too. "And you saw my car number yesterday before leaving for home." asked Anant.

"No sir actually I noticed it when you arrived the night before." replies the boy. "Ok, so why can't I go to south I mean to Delhi?" asked Rohit.

"Because there was another landslide before Dharampur on the way to Delhi, which is not cleared." replies boy.

This was unexpected NEWS for Anant, who had to there at Delhi for a meeting. "Can I do anything else for you." asked the hotel boy. "That was really kind replied Anant, I will call you when I need help." said Anant. And the boy leaves the room and shut the room behind.

Anant powered on the television, and set it to NEWS channel in order to get the latest update. But the NEWS says that the work is in progress, and it will take almost twenty four hours to resume the traffic to the normal. He is struck here for more than a day now.

He went to the switch board and unplugged his mobile phone, which is considerably charged. Anant presses the power button to switch on the mobile. The LCD of the mobile gets bright with the colors and suddenly it went dark again. Anant again tried to power on his mobile by pressing the power button but same is the result. Anant's mobile is spoiled as it suffered a fall from couch, when he was sleeping the last night.

Anant have to inform Rohit about landslide and his inconvenience to reach Delhi for today's meeting, but as per now he don't have any possible way for that and he don't even remember Rohit's contact number so that he could call him, all he can do is wait till evening for basketball practice, and will call Rohit, from Ritika's mobile.

17

Nature's way

The breath rate of Anant is near to eighty breaths per minute, and his lungs trying everything they have to breathe as fast they can. He is jogging back to his hotel room, after evening basketball practice with the kids. He thought Ritika would be there and he would use her mobile phone to call Rohit. But she dint turned up.

Anant is not able to digest the absence of Ritika on the basketball court, he remember that she had invited him to the basketball court, with the condition if he somehow does not leave Shimla. He is thinking, 'she invited me and she herself did not turned up, maybe there is something wrong with her.' When he enquired about her absence from the kids who were playing with him, he came to know that usually she comes to play every day, there would have been a reason why she did not turned up today.

The running legs comes to rest, Anant looks at the street on his left, it is the same street which he and Ritika travelled together yesterday to Ritika's home. He wants make a visit to Ritika to confirm that she is fine. He looks at the street towards his left, thinks for a while and finally smiles and resumes his jogging on the main road, towards his hotel.

Anant's body is sweating even in this freezing cold, but his feet at run. Anant cuts the speed off as he reaches the hotel. But instead of entering the hotel, he again stands at the valley side of the road and limbers his breath down. Anant again looks at the deep valley, which is still filled with snow.

Today he is not concern about the beauty of valley, but his concerns lies with Ritika and his decision not to take the road to her home. He is still not sure why did he not went to her home, may be because he dint want to make her feel wired, as it has been one day they have meat after so long and it would be weird to knock the gate of someone without prior information, or may be because he is feeling something for her which he did not want to.

Anant is meshed up with his thoughts and he himself is not sure what he is feeling. But one thing is clear that something is different in him, the thing which was making him mad since last four months; no longer have any effective influence on him now. Adhilisha is most probably married and he should be broken by even thought of this, but instead he is thinking of Ritika.

After few minutes of time with himself, he turns and moves in the hotel premises after crossing the road. As he enters the main hotel building, one of the same girls at the reception called him, and gave him one paper and said: "A lady came to see you, when we told her that you are not in your room, she left this message for you." she said.

In Shimla except Ritika, no one knows him and he knew the lady the receptionist is talking is Ritika. "Thank you." said Anant and is about to leave but the receptionist hand over another paper, "we received a call from Mr. Rohit, he said he is friend of yours and he is trying to contact you but could not, he had send this fax for you." Anant collected the fax and moves towards his room.

After entering in his room Anant switches on the television, set it to NEWS channel, and then lies down on the couch. He had played basketball for an hour or so and jogged back to hotel, this is enough to drain him out of energy. His muscles are getting cold and he can feel the lactic acid in his thighs and back. The NEWS says that, the work to clear the landslide near Dharampur is still in progress. After listing to this he picked the remote of his television and closed it.

He places the remote on the table and looks at the fax which has only three lines printed, Anant starts reading the fax from Rohit, it says:

'I tried to contact you on your mobile but it is switched off. I heard in NEWS about the landslide, you don't worry about things here I will handle them all. And Adhilisha got married last night. You take care.'

The news of Adhilisha's marriage is not showing much difference on Anant, may be because he was ready and well prepared for it, or may be because he is liking this place more than usual.

Then he took the sheet which was left for him by a lady, the sheet says:

'Hay, I am realllllyyyy sry that I could not make to Basketball court, I was caught by work in bank today. Let's meat at eight in evening on mall road, will be waiting for you. If you have other plans call me at my number."

And the message ends with contact number and name of individual who has written the message as Ritika.

Anant looks at his watch and it is ten minutes to six. Enough time and he can rest his body for a while. The pleasure of lying when you are extremely tired is something inexpressible. He is just lying on couch and resting his back but when sleep took over him, he dint came to knew.

His sleep is interfered by the voice of inter-com, he stretches his hand to receive the call but he still is under the smoke of sleep. It is receptionist on other side of the call, she tells him that someone name Ritika is here to see you, his eyes gets wide open and he is pushed out of sleep immediately. Anant looks at his watch it is around nine. He asks the receptionist to hand over the phone to Ritika.

Receptionist hands over the phone to Ritika, immediately after Greetings were exchanged Anant asked her to wait for a minute and he will be there and she agreed.

Anant immediately places the receiver and in a flash of seconds he wears his shoes, washes his face, and takes a dip in perfume as he came smell his order and runs to the reception.

Ritika's eyes are on the stairs looking for Anant, she is quite annoyed by Anant's behavior. She was waiting for Anant at mall road for more than half an hour and was positive of Anant's arrival as she did not received any information from Anant about alteration in the plan. She had left her contact number in the message that she had left for Anant at the reception, so that Anant could inform her of any change in program, but neither he informed and nor he turned to Mall road.

Finally Ritika saw Anant walking down the stairs

No greeting but the first words that came from Ritika's mouth is: "you alive, I thought it contrary." As she is quite annoyed of Anant's behavior,

"I am really sorry, I dint even came to know when I was slept." said Anant. Anant continued: "and I am paying for my mistake today's dinner is on me."

Finally Ritika smiles, she tried but she could not be angry from Anant for too long, and says: "apologies accepted and the venue for dinner will be decided by me." Anant nodes in positive with a smile and Ritika continue, "And we are having dinner first, as I am feeling hungry and then we can roam at Mall road." Anant smiled and said, "As you command mam."

"So let's get in your car, the roads are clear we can drive there." said Ritika. Anant responds with a smile, and then they both went to the parking. Anant opens the front door of car for her, but instead of occupying the seat Ritika said: "You occupy the seat dear, I am driving." Anant hands the keys to her and occupies the seat and closes the door. While Ritika move around the car and opens the doors and enters the car. She ignites the engines and they are on move.

Anant and Ritika are on the Mall road and till now they have not eaten anything. Anant is feeling hungry and so did Ritika is. Anant don't know where they are going

for dinner, he had already asked Ritika twice, but both times she asked him to have patience.

"Would you like to have starters' first or direct meal?" asked Ritika.

Anant could not get her questions, they are on Road and this question may have made sense when they would have been in any restaurant but as they are moving on the road this question holds no importance. While Anant is thinking how to respond to this question asked by Ritika, she spoke again, "You dint replied to my question, Starters' or not."

Anant still dint know how to respond, but usually he prefers starters so he replies: "Yes I would prefer starters."

Ritika smiles after listening to his reply and took him by his arm and moves towards a Gool Gappe stall, and said let's start with the starters. Anant did not assume this to be in starters but he is happy that finally he is having something.

The shopkeeper gave them two plates, one to each and asked for the taste of water they would like to have, Anant said sweet and Ritika said spicy. After two pieces were served Anant feels his stomach burning he looks at Ritika, she seems to be fine. Ritika looks at him and says with a smile on her face: "yummy na!" Anant see the smile on Ritika's face it is the like flowers in the freezing cold. Before Anant could respond the shopkeeper places another piece in his plate, he took it and ate it and hick ups breaks.

Ritika immediately ran to next shop and brought a mineral water bottle. She opens the cap of bottle and hand it over to Anant. Anant immediately drank water from it, his hick ups are cured but due to spice, water is running from his eyes. Finding Anant in a fine state Ritika resumes her Gool Gappe.

Ritika ends with her Gool Gappe and the ones which were left by Anant. Anant pays the money and turns back to Ritika who is standing behind him. Ritika asks for water bottle from him, and they start to move on the Mall road ahead. Anant hand over the bottle to Ritika; she opens the bottle and starts to drink from it.

Anant have a different smile on his face since Ritika bought the mineral water bottle for him, Anant is looking at Ritika, she is drinking water and he smiles wider. Ritika asked him after drinking water that why he is smiling. Listening to her Anant could not hold him and laughed out loud.

Ritika is surprised to see Anant laughing so weirdly. She again asks him, what is going on. Anant controls his laughter, relaxes the muscles of his face and begin: "when I was getting hick ups you ran for water."

Ritika nods in acceptance, Anant continues: "and you ran to another shop to purchase a mineral water bottle.

Dint you saw a pot at your side, you could have given me that water."

"The water in the pot was not purified and would have caused health effects." replies Ritika. "And you think the water he prepared for Gool Gappe was made from purified water and will keep you healthy." said Anant and he laughs again.

Anant and Ritika roamed on the mall road and had street food, which was full of spices and Anant could feel his stomach burning. It is twenty one hours and thirty minutes; the shops at mall road are mostly closed, and hardly anyone is visible on the mall road, the temperature had dipped sharply below minus eight degrees and expected to fall further as night gets deep. Their cloths are running on lower side to keep them safe from cold.

They plans to move to Ridge where they can sit and thought they will find people too.

If we move up on mall road it ends at ridge. The ridge is a beautiful open place, and is called the heart of Shimla. The jewels of Ridge are, a church built in neo-Gothic style, a Tudorbethan-styled library building, a fountain and plenty of open space.

Its full moon tomorrow, but still the night is dark because of presence of clouds. But luckily for Anant these clouds are not precipitating. The glimpse of moon becomes possible when it peeps between the gaps of clouds and the queen of mountains gets visible, an amazing view with mountains all around covered with snow, but as soon as the queen is visible in her new white attire the clouds blocks the lights again.

Anant's back and thighs are showing the effect of lactic acid but his knee is fine as its special care is taken by bandage. He wants to go hotel but when he looks at Ritika, he finds happiness on her face which he does not want to spoil. So they both kept on moving towards the Ridge, walking right in between of the road full of snow and no one is visible around or anything in this case, because of clouds, all that is visible is these two alone cut from the rest of the world moving together.

Anant and Ritika reach the Ridge, but contrary to what they thought, they did not found anyone here too. They covered the open space and reach the fountain, which obvious is not flowing in this cold. The temperature is reaching negative nine degree among the lowest ever recorded. They sits at the step of the fountain, the floor is so frozen that it feels like sitting on the slab of ice cube. But as few minutes pass the temperature of floor gets balanced.

It's been more than ten minutes for them here but they had are hardly talking to each other, it look like the talking part is done by nature between them. The voice of freezing air making its way from the trees is loud and audible but louder than air they can hear the sound of their own hearts which are running like untamed houses.

The cold breeze is not in a mood to give up and rather it is switching to romantic mood, to get some warmth they both got close and squeezes more into each other. That is not all from breeze; it goes more wild and strong, Anant looks at Ritika she is squeezing and rubbing her hands to get warmth, Anant took her left hand into his left hand locks his fingers into hers and his right hand around her shoulders which bought her more near to him.

Ritika looks into his eyes and Anant too is looking into hers. Ritika is feeling some different kind of force in her and her heart is pumping faster than ever. She took a long deep breath, closes her eyes and her lower lip rubs with her upper lip, Anant could feel the grip of Ritika's hand grip getting stronger at his hand. She exhaled from her mouth and rested her head at Anant's shoulder.

Few minutes passes like this, now nature is not only speaking between them but acting too. The natural feelings and thoughts have unleashed in their brains. Their breath is uncomfortably raised, Anant is feeling something which he is not able to control even after his beat efforts finally he says "I think we should move now, it's late and uncomfortably cold." Ritika looks at him and nods.

Ritika raises her head from Anant's shoulder and Anant releases Ritika's hand and Anant raises and forwards his hand for Ritika to take and stand up, she took his hand and Ritika too stood up. Then they start to cross the Ridge towards the Mall road.

Nature have its own ways, you can run from it but can't escape. At the end nature will always find a way, as nature had found a way here.

They reach the center of the Ridge, Ritika holds Anant's both hands and stands in front of him with her eyes into his. Ritika takes a step close to Anant; they are so close that they can hear each other's breath. Ritika raises her neck and closes her eyes Anant leans forward, grabs her in his arms and kisses her.

18

A New Road

$\mathcal{E}$arly seven in the morning and Anant is under the shower in his hotel room. An unusual time for Anant to wake up, but the last night had been restless. He was awake twice in his short sleep. Something unexpected had happened last night, when he was with Ritika at Mall road and he doesn't know how to respond to it, he is not able to decide whether to run from it or to embrace it.

His head is down and body leaning towards the front wall with his hands on the wall and the water is directly falling on his shoulders and head.

It is a peaceful and silent morning; just the sound made by the water from the shower can be heard. Peace could be felt all around and but a turmoil is going in head of Anant. He is not able to decide what is happening to him, Adhilisha was love of his life, without her he never imagined his life and neither wanted it to be. The pain of her absence and feelings, which were corroding him slowly from inside have suddenly, lost their effect on him.

On the contrary Ritika is causing more problems to him, he is attracted towards her and what happened yesterday is something he himself could not give explanations. It all happened in a gust of flow of feelings but some part of him is not accepting all this.

Anant raises his head and now water is directly on his face, he wiped his face with his hands, takes a step backward, stops the shower and turns towards the mirror which is on the left side of the powder room. He stares at himself for a while, but could not recognize the man in the mirror; something is happening to him that he does not want to accept or he is over thinking. He turns and wears the gown and leaves the wash room.

Anant enters the main hall and switch on the television. All the NEWS channels are oozing out with the voices of Pandits, who are yelling at their voice to tell there viewers that how there day will proceed and what all they need to do to make it better. But Anant have no interest in hearing their prophecy and neither have any interest in the television for now. He switched the television on as he had nothing to do and want some kind of diversion.

He start to flips the channels and finally stops at a music channel, luckily he founded what he wanted 'the rock music'. He increases the volume, loud enough for music to take over him, and it worked too. Soon Anant is murmuring the song and he is out of thoughts of everything.

Anant calls for beer and the beer added to the comfort of Anant. Anant is two bottles down and reaches to the balcony with another bottle in his hand. He opens the window, it is comfortably cold outside. He steps out in balcony, opens the cap of the beer, and takes few sips and now looking at the valley.

The valley is still covered with snow and is lifeless, it is third day of Anant here in Shimla, and sun has kept itself away from the queen of hills. It is 8:30 in the morning and Anant's eyes find the traffic on the road. The traffic may be because the way to Delhi may have resumed or may be because of the traffic in the Shimla that was resumed yesterday. But he is not in the hurry to confirm the reason of traffic on the road as he has plans for evening. He stands on the balcony and enjoys valley, cold and beer.

'When love strikes someone the diversions does not keep them diverted and happy for too long.' The effect of beer and music is down and the thoughts of Ritika are up again. Anant wants to talk to Rohit about what all happened and what all are happening to him, because Rohit is his best friend and understands him. And who in the world could advise him better than Rohit. But he does not have any convince to get in touch with Rohit, this time he himself has to face all this alone.

Anant finishes his third beer and enters the room, where he uses the intercom to call the room service, to order one more beer. After few minutes a boy with beer enters the room. Anant asks him to place the beer on the table in front of the couch. The boy does same and then asks for his leave, Anant pays his thanks by a hundred rupee note to him. When the boy is about to leave the room something sticks to Anant's brain, he asks the boy to hold, the boy turns back and says: "yes sir what else I can do for you."

Anant asks him about the highway to Delhi, the boy tells him that the highway is cleared from snow and traffic had resumed. The boy leaves.

Now a new problem generates, yesterday when Anant left Ritika to her flat, he promised her that they will meet in evening for dinner at mall road today. Now the traffic had resumed and he should move to Delhi. He slowly drinks beer and thinks on what he should do now.

Anant is at the reception of the hotel where he was staying and now he is checking out. He pays his bills and move towards the parking where his car is waiting for him. A boy from the hotel carries his luggage behind him to the car.

During the day Anant had a sleep of few hours after he was done with the beers, as he is planning to leave for Delhi tonight, after dinner with Ritika. The dinner is planned at nine in the evening, and it is already twenty passed eight. And Anant still have to start his journey towards the Oberoi Wildflower, where he will meet Ritika for dinner.

Oberoi Windflower is the best Hotel in Shimla, Situated 8,250 feet above in the magnificent Himalayas, the beauty of the hotel could not be expressed in the words but could only be felt.

Anant enters his dark color BMW X3 (F25), ignites the engine and moves towards Windflower, where he had a table already booked for him and Ritika.

It is ten minutes to nine and Ritika is already sitting at Windflower, waiting for Anant to come. She was so excited for this dinner that she could not wait for clock to show 21:00 hours. She already had waited for twenty minutes and still ten minutes are to pass and but she is enjoying waiting.

Ritika took an off from her office today, and spend the whole day in shopping perfect dress for the dinner. She is wearing a deep red color gown, accompanied with two and half inch high white Nude Pumps but the Nude Pumps are not visible under the gown. Actually she purchased the Pumps first and then she went to purchase the dress, one peace top was in her brain but she ended up with the gown, this usually happens we plan something and we end up in purchasing something else. Pumps are not visible but they are adding to the height of Ritika and making her look mesmerizing tall and beautiful. She wanted to look special on the dinner and she is looking more than special.

It is five minutes to nine and Anant enters the Wildflower Hall, where Ritika is waiting for him. He joins Ritika on the table; Ritika is looking ravishing and could not stop himself from giving a compliment to her. Ritika smile wide and accepts the greeting with thanks, her labor for the day is paid off.

And after exchange of normal talks they order food and vine. While they are in the middle of the dinner, Anant says: "I have to say something."

Ritika knows what is coming now; this is what she was waiting for. She acted as if she does not know anything and says: "Ya, I am listening."

Rohit pulls out the same ring case which he had bought to purpose Adhilisha for marriage, from his jeans. Places it on the table and open the case.

Ritika is speechless to see a beautiful ring in front of her. She is so happy that she wants to jump out from the chair, but she is just holding her excitement to hear those three words from Anant. She was thinking that Anant may say her that, he use to like her during the school days, or he likes her now, or they could be friends forever, or in the best case he would have said that he love her, but a proposal for marriage she never expected.

But at last she is happy to see what is happening and her dreams are getting into shape.

Anant says: "four months ago I purchased this ring to propose my girlfriend, but was never able to propose her, as we parted."

Suddenly all the dreams of Ritika breaks, and she don't know how to behave now.

Anant continues: "and she got married two nights before."

Ritika is thinking why is he telling me all this but did not interfered in between.

Anant added further: "i was not able to handle my feelings after she left me, and was just breathing but not leaving, until me meat you here. I seriously don't know what to say now. I like your company," a long pause and Ritika is still looking at him, she is not sure what exactly he wants to come up with.

"i bought this ring here for you, will you take it."

"With pleasure" replies Ritika, and takes the ring.

"And don't forget we are best friends, and will always remain best friends even if the world turns against us" replies Ritika. And Anant nods and says, "Always."

After the dinner Anant, is on the way to Ritika's home where he will drop her and after dropping her Anant will leave for Delhi.

They reach Ritika's home, and Anant parks the car at the side of street. Anant says: "So we will be meeting soon, I believe."

Ritika replies: "Do let me know about your next tour to Shimla, and I will tell you if I have any plans to Delhi."

"But how will you tell me about your plans to visit Delhi, you don't have my contact number" replies Anant.

Ritika: "Mr. Intelligent, I will get it from Rohit." And they laugh.

Ritika moves towards him and hugs him, and whisper in his ear "keep in touch."

Ritika leaves the car and smiles and says, "take care on the way, captain."

Anant smiles and says: "you too" and he starts to drive the car. He is looking at the rare view mirror; Ritika is still standing outside and looking at the car.

Standing and watching Anant to leave, she is thinking, 'not a bad start, hope the future may be good between us.'

Anant is on the way back to Delhi, it's been half an hour since he had dropped Ritika at her flat. It is 00:00 hours, its full moon tonight but again clouds in their colors, and a dark road ahead, now Anant knows where his life is going now, he is travelling on a new road towards new life, in his old car.

His eyes are caught by the dashboard of his car, some not new but still fresh memories retrieves.

Anant opens the dashboard takes the ring case. The ring case is empty as he had gifted the ring to Ritika. He places the Box in front of him; smiles while looking at box and whispers to himself:

> "I never allowed my thoughts,
> to be free from her.
> I still have her with me,
> but now she doesn't."

And Abhay vanishes ahead on new road.